Nia

Nia

Robert Minhinnick

Seren is the book imprint of
Poetry Wales Press Ltd
57 Nolton Street, Bridgend, Wales, CF31 3AE
www.serenbooks.com
Facebook: facebook.com/SerenBooks
Twitter: @SerenBooks

ISBNs
Paperback – 978-1-78172-550-4
Ebook – 978-1-78172-551-1
Kindle – 978-1-78172-552-8

A CIP record for this title is available from the British Library.

The publisher acknowledges the financial assistance of the Welsh
Books Council.

Cover Illustration: Aristolochia clematitis, 1885

Printed in Bembo by Severn, Gloucester, UK.

Nia

I

Hence, viper thoughts, that coil around my mind,
Reality's dark dream!

It was a hot day and she was gazing into the sun. There was a dog far away and she realised she was looking at it.

Now she was walking towards the dog, past an apple tree and through the grass. This was a familiar place and she was happy here but she was going to see what the dog was doing, that dog with the blaze on its chest and white on its tail.

The dog was staring at her and she was staring at the dog and then they were together and she realized it was a fox. The biggest fox she had ever encountered in the dunes. A fox with a white tail.

And as she reached the fox it bared its teeth and these were bloody. Bleeding, its teeth, or maybe the fox had been eating another creature. Blood on its lips and its jaw red. Blood on its breast.

II

It's… *malarial*, said Skye to Nia. Dry week after dry week.

Malaria runs in my family. Yes. *Scorchio*. As they say.

Summer dresses are just walking out of here, laughed Serene. If only we were charging more…

We're not cashing in, insisted Nia. We're not supporting sweatshops…Remember, everything we sell tells a story. It's up to us to make those stories known…

And be sure Lois is up to date, added Skye.

Lois was the Saturday girl who'd been taken on recently. She was proving successful at attracting custom and was also eager to babysit.

That story about the mats was great, smiled Nia.

Yeah?

Made only by men? While not using electricity? That was a new one on me. I did a separate blog about that.

Which was perfect, said Skye. *Product of the week* is a superb idea. Pity we can't choose more.

I like the offcuts from the saris, added Serene. All the things they become! Incredible.

*

They had been talking in the shop. When Isaac Pretty arrived they moved on to the fairground. Here, Nia had bought her daughter candyfloss. Then the child had been taken home by Serene and the other three gone to the caravans in The Backs.

What do they call you? asked Skye.

Marshals, said Rizmas.

Marshals?

Bit American, isn't it? laughed Ike.

But first, said Nia, where's Virjilijs?

Gone home, said Rizmas. Met a girl. Also, this referendum thing. Says maybe he'll be back. Next week. Don't know how. Anyway, Petr's still here.

So you're in charge of The Sunflower? The new ride?

The Star Chaser? You might call it something different.

Oh, we have our own names for things, said Nia.

Well, Petr's working today. Me tonight. Hey, I've been here three years...I'm senior, I'm...

A marshal, laughed Ike. Yes, it's all changed now. Surprised they haven't given you a badge.

But not changed here yet, shrugged Rizmas, gesturing around the caravan. This was parked in the network of passageways behind the fairground.

Is it scheduled? asked Nia. I mean for development?

They say they will knock this place down, said Rizmas. Next year. Year after. They say it's all change in the fair. They say. But who knows? Not me.

Three years? asked Ike.

This my third summer.

Enjoying the weather?

So different from last year. Fantastic. Sometimes Petr and I sleep out, and always we leave the door open. Stinks in here. Sorry.

The visitors looked round. The caravan walls were hung with cuttle carvings strung on nylon fishing line. There were lead weights and pieces of driftwood also hanging, as if it was a schoolroom displaying children's art. Shelves were filled with stones veined with quartz while fronds of seaweed were fixed above the door.

Rizmas looked at his visitors as they stared. Petr, sometimes he complains, he smiled. Yes. Says please, please don't bring anything else from the beach. From the big stones.

The Horns? asked Nia. You go up there?

Oh, I walk around, I walk around. I walk and I work. Mostly work. One hundred hours last week…

Money good? asked Skye.

That's why I'm here. But I tell Petr, I say, you know the sea. You know the Baltic. But not me. I never saw the sea till I came here. I never saw the Baltic. Look, I'm from the east and I was born in the trees. The forests there last forever…

So you miss the forest?

This is better. This is amazing to me. I never dreamed anywhere like it.

It's you collect the stones? And carve cuttle?

Yes. And Petr, he gets used to it now…

It's wonderful, said Skye, running her forefinger down a tawse of yellow weed. I feel I'm in church. What do you carve with?

Rizmas took down a knife from the shelf. Okay, Petr told

me not to carry it on the rides. But people can be, can be…
strange…

Oh yes, we know, smiled Nia. *Aggravating* is the word. When
we were the Paradise Club I kept certain things handy under
the counter…My own cudgel. Boy, I love that word!

But not now, laughed Skye. It's a different clientele. Okay,
some boys on the weekends can be stupid.

Booze, said Nia. You know.

Yes, since the hours are longer, said Rizmas. Usually the
last ride finishes in the dark… Not supposed to, but…

Long hours, said Skye.

But everyone was looking at Rizmas. They saw it was a
flick knife he was holding, fine as a stiletto. The boy picked
up a piece of cuttle and peeled off a sliver.

Yes, some people can be very strange. When they come out
of The Cat. But I know what to do. Petr and me are watch-
ful…

Rizmas stood beside a sofa covered with a sleeping bag.
There were clothes and dirty plates on the floor and pages
torn from a spiral-bound notebook. An empty spirit bottle
emblazoned with '999' lay in a corner, another on a shelf. In
the opposite corner was the head of a carousel horse, upon it
the name *Sylvia* ornate in worn gold.

The boy flicked upon the stiletto. Then he closed it. Then
he flicked it open again.

He was naked to the waist, his jeans, bleached and torn,
held up by a belt with a snake's head fastening. The hair on
his chest was white over a brown skin, once burnt and peeling,

now darkened again. His hair also was white, long and flat and pale as the cuttlebone he carved. On his right bicep was the tattoo, *Ironwolves*.

Rizmas was lean and muscled, not a surplus ounce. Nia noted a white scar on his belly.

Fair play, you've stuck it, she said.

In a way, like home. For me, Kaunas was the big city. You know Kaunas?

Always meant to…started Ike.

Kaunas very famous. Used to be flights over.

It's changing, said Skye.

All my friends liked Kaunas. We went there on the weekends.

Bit like here, said Nia.

Yes. It's the same. In a way. Kaunas was famous because of the museum.

No museum here, man, said Skye.

No, a special museum. The devil's museum.

Yeah?

Yes. When I went I always looked at the devil's vodka glass.

Drank vodka, did he? laughed Ike.

And his fingerprint, no, the print of his thumb was on the glass.

Yeah?

Because he's hot. The devil. He drank the vodka and his fingers melted the glass. Everybody knows that. So…

So you've come to the devil's museum on The Caib, said Nia.

Yes. I work on the rides. But in the mornings I sweep the mess in the Ghost Train. Next door to the Ghost Train is...

The Kingdom of Evil, said Nia.

Yes. Sweep all kinds of things. Dirty things.

Ha, said Ike. All the debris of copulation?

Cop..?

Oh, I can imagine, said Nia. You wouldn't believe what I have to sweep up outside the shop.

And me, said Skye. Not just you...

But... Rizmas stuttered. Don't get me wrong...

When I stepped off the last bus, at the bus stop by the entrance, I smelled the air. And, you know I had never smelled anything like that air before. Not spruce trees, no way. Better...

Yes, the sea, said Ike.

I looked up and there it was. A silver line. My first time. The tide was far away. A kilometre across the beach. And the sky was white, not like now. White like cuttlefish.

Can be a big cuttle harvest around here, said Nia.

Hey, said Ike. Did the devil drink triple nine?

Maybe the question went unheard by everyone but Nia.

That mummy's a real museum piece, she said. I had to wind its bandages back on, once. There was all this gooey stuff used to stick them on.

Embalming fluid, said Skye.

And, oh God, the hounds of hell. Manky old taxidermist's nightmares. Falling to bits...

But they're not even stuffed, said Skye.

No. Course not. They're not real. Kind of paper pulp.

13

Painted over and over. But historic in their way.

Well, said Skye, I would hate to see that decrepit Franken-stein's monster in the skip. He's an antique.

A bloody stripper bolt through his neck, said Ike. Who the hell...?

And Igor, the hound master, said Skye. But I think Igor's kept inside.

Yeah, said Ike. So as not to disappoint anyone. You've already paid your dosh before you meet Igor.

Never heard of anyone getting their money back, said Nia. Point of honour not to cough up. But that's our museum. Can't remember if there's a devil in the ghost train. Not drink-ing vodka, anyway. Now, a pint of woosh, maybe.

But a vodka glass! laughed Skye. Think that's sexier than just filling your face. Which is what most of the men around here do.

I love it, said Rizmas. Everything the sea gives us is, is...

A gift? suggested Nia.

Yes, yes. But it was salt I could smell. The air full of salt. And sand. And every day I smell it again, every day when I wake up, either here or under the new ride because sometimes it is better to sleep out. Especially when it is hot. And because Petr snores like, like...

A donkey? suggested Nia.

Donkey, yes. Who give rides on the beach. Those donkeys, we work like those donkeys. I'll tell Petr that... But it's better here. Better than sorting rubbish at the incinerator. One of the other boys is doing that... He says it is terrible in this hot weather. No air and his uniform not right… But every day, the first thing for me to notice is…the smell of The Caib.

Yeah. We know, said Ike.

But not chips. Not the outfall pipe. No, the salt of high tide, low tide, it doesn't matter. And the salt of The Caib in my eyes. Every morning my eyes stuck with salt… We have a bucket of water to bathe in and that's first thing for me, bathing my eyes. So I can see again. Or, I go to the showers.

Yeah, said Ike, glancing round. Who are the *Ironwolves*?

Video game, Rizmas said. We don't have one in the arcades here. It is popular at home…But so much money the people here have for the machines. They start every morning till late at night. I watch them, sometimes I help bag the coins if the boss asks.

You don't bank it, do you?

No, someone else.

You must like that game a lot, laughed Ike.

Who's the boss? asked Nia.

Mr Manners is big boss. Other little bosses.

Oh well, yeah, said Nia. Because there's money around, I know it. Pity they never come over to *Extraordinaria*. It's hardly far. Not very adventurous our locals. More's the pity.

III

'Tis midnight, but small thoughts have I of sleep:
Full seldom may my friend such vigils keep!'

The seagulls. So early. Unearthly, the seagulls... But get thee... get thee to...

What the hell, John Vine again, using other people's words... Shakespeare wasn't it? A man's voice in her head. Her father's, in that Year Thirteen play.

She turned in the bed.No, he'd never knowingly hurt her. Never that. But she was going to find him. Find John Vine.

And there had really been a nunnery, people said, under the sands. There were the ruins of a mill, a firing range, and...maybe a nunnery, or at least its garden. Somewhere lost, though she'd once been able to discover it.But once only. Like so much she couldn't find now.

So she lay waiting for Ffresni to wake.Ffrez curled up in bed, under the driftwood mobile.The murmur on the child's lips gentler than breath.

4a.m. First daylight. Mother of pearl between the blinds and the cockerel again, the cockerel that had crowed before dawn, had called in the darkness.

No it wasn't the gulls, don't blame the seagulls, it was the first cockerel she had heard on The Caib for years.Kept in a back garden down Cato Street. Because things were changing. It wasn't only the heat.

But yes, the heat... And those flowers, she'd once found the flowers.How many years ago? Lifetimes it seemed. But they'd come back to her mind so clearly. Rare, weren't they? Protected? Strange yellow flowers with stranger fruits. Flowers in the shape of the...shape of the birth canal, she'd read. Shape of the...uterus then? Those weird flowers with their peculiar fruit... But evidence, surely, of that nunnery of legend.

The nuns planted those flowers, hadn't they? And the flowers were there still, lost in the dunes, lost in the... Yet birth canal, what a strange way to describe a flower. But poisonous too, those blooms, their strange smell of what... The afterbirth?

Ach, sex nauseous. Sex noxious.The flowers stank of sex. And still here, those flowers, hundreds of years later. After the nuns had gone, their poison flowers remained. She'd found them once but couldn't say where... But they were exactly where she thought they'd be. Thank God, she had discovered them.

So maybe they dosed themselves, those nuns, aborting their own children. Just as chastity aborted their dreams... Or even allowed those dreams to flourish. Clever, weren't they, the nuns? Who knew more than you'd think. Busy as wrens in their brown habits. Their brown rags. Yes, there they were, cowled and hungry, testing themselves. Enduring that hunger.

But worst
the atrocity of thirst

Ha! But women tending their herbs and the veins purple in the old nuns' hands.Testing themselves. What happens to old nuns? Such brave women.

But vanished now and their garden gone wild. And those flowers that smelled of…

Golden trumpets, she had thought. On the one occasion she had needed to search…. Yes, golden trumpets…

*

Skye regarded the goat. Its agate eye. Young nanny, not long from a kid. Then her beard, black lip and nubbins of horns. The goat was scattering pellets like seed over the straw. Quickly she photographed the face. Black and white, she thought. Yes, a beautiful child. Becoming a ruined god.

Meanwhile, Nia was dropping feed into the chute and now the goat was ravenous, trying to lick the grains before Big Mama came over and claimed her rights. Big Mama with her shitty arse and some kind of prolapse, Big Mamma even now nudging the younger goat out of the straw around the trough.

Yes, here's the greedy one, said Nia. Now Ffrez, you do it, you feed the goats. And the child let her handful slip into the chute as the goats' hooves skidded in the pen. Nia brushed hair over a mark on the child's forehead.

That's right, love.

Good, Ffresni, added Skye.

Goats are greedy, aren't they? You greedy goats!

The three had driven over to Hafn Bitw, now a petting zoo. Once a derelict farm, it had been leased to a family who were making the venture work. Prefabricated additions had been attached to the outbuildings.

The three had used Skye's Mazda and parked where they could. Fine weather had made Hafn Bitw popular but Nia had been coughing in the field's dust. She noted the buzzing in her head again. Could she have tinnitus in one ear?

Next were the pigs. There were two in a sty further up the field, two sows, like the goats, one younger, the other dominant, one capable of nipping the other, making it squeal.

Skye looked into the first pig's eyes. Sly in the clefts, the mean creases. Cold cinders, those eyes. That yet might flare. What was buried there so deeply? In a pig's eyes.

Fear, she guessed. And was it boredom? The boredom of being a pig? No, pigs in shit were happy pigs. And always a view to the main chance.

Ffresni was again allowed to throw a handful of food into the chute.

Ooh, Nia laughed. Like a strawberry in a sow's belly. That's what they used to say, isn't it?

Who used to say? asked Skye.

Well, not you. The elders in Clwb y Mor, bless 'em. Means something...*insubstantial*.

Elders? Jeez.

Committee, then.

Codgers were they?

Trustees. That's the word.

But Skye had put down her camera. The pigs' eyes were buried in creases like coin slots. Old blackberries, she thought. That had lost their blush. Not goat's eyes with a sulphuric gleam, where the intelligence shone through.

Not that she might trust a goat. A sphinx, that goat. Yet a god's sacrificial throat.

Now the pigs were tearing at one another and Ffresni looking frightened. Ahead were the Shetland ponies but the women decided to detour to the rabbits.

Nia thought about the animals that didn't emerge from their huts. The runts preferring darkness. Or the trembling farrow chewing pissed-on hay.

Coffee? suggested Skye.

Mmm...

Not that I can take pictures inside. Regulations and all.

I'll just show Ffrez about washing her hands. They're dead keen on this with children. She touched the guinea pig, after all.

They walked across the crushed grass. The coffee shop was located in the indoor area. There were no animals here but chances for children to play. A plastic slide had been set up, a track for toy cars, ringed by tyres, and two rooms that might be hired for private parties. Only two of the restaurant tables were occupied.

Are you scared? asked Nia.

Of what?

Going down. Where we're going.

Course not. Are you?

No. But...

It's 100% safe. There's Ffrez, I know. But look, Serene is wonderful with her... And if it's only Ffresni? Which is natural. But anything else?

What you mean, only Ffrez?

There's nothing else bothering you?

I've decided, haven't I?

Well really it was your idea…

Look. I'd die for her.

Yes, but…

Here and now. No buts. I'd die for her. And you haven't…

Haven't…?

Got…

Look, said Skye, reaching for Nia's hand. I know. I understand. But, yes, Ffrez. Of course Ffrez. And the shop doing so well this summer.

Well…

There was a pause. Nia slowly brightened.

Remember that woman who bought four dresses one afternoon last week. But then brought two of them back the next day…

So it goes, said Skye. But that cupboard you distressed last year went a fortnight ago.

Yes, that's good. Ooh, doesn't she like that little house. Putting the toy chairs around the table…Picking up the plastic flowers.

Must be in our genes, laughed Skye.

Tidying up, sort of, smiled Nia.

Her hair's getting thicker. And long.

Not cutting it, said Nia. No way.

Who's asking you to? Hey, calm down…

Don't niggle then.

Who's niggling?

Mentioning dresses brought back...

Look, we've popped out for this treat, said Skye. Don't let's argue. Again. We both need to get ready after we go back...

There was a pause.

Zugzwang. Again, said Nia.

What? asked Skye.

When one of us doesn't want to speak.

Why?

Because when we speak it's bound to be wrong.

Zugs..?

Used in chess. When one side must move but that move will weaken its chances.

Oh.

Chess is life to some people.

Not you though.

No.

And not us.

Ulrikke.

Who?

The computer I play against. There's a choice of voices and Ulrikke's a Norwegian nymphet. Very Scandi noir. Or something like that. But no.

And not us.

Nia smiled. These days that was infrequent. Look, she said, if the computer's winning, I change things.

How?

Make it more stupid. I think it's one till eight. On the gauge, that is. Eight is most difficult. But the better the computer plays, the slower it moves. So I get bored. I stay on three. Because I like to play fast. And sometimes I know when the computer is getting desperate.

Do computers get...?

Okay, okay, it's not possible. People get desperate. Not machines. But Ulrikke makes mistakes. Makes sacrifices just to slow things up. To delay the inevitable. My victory, her loss. But she already understands the inevitable. When that happens I really like it... A little triumph. But...

Yes?

Using sacrifice as strategy seems alien to the computer.

Is that good?

Yes. Sacrifice is all too human. Isn't it?

Skye made a face and looked away. Don't play enough chess, do I? Suppose you've got to be...proficient to understand sacrifice.

There was a pause. At last, Skye spoke.

Ike's double-checking the gear. I hope.

Trust him?

Yeah, yeah. He wasn't always trustworthy, you know. No, don't ask. But look at Ffrez, oh, she's putting the cups away now. In her own fashion. But did you think you'd be doing that for Carpenter...?

Tidying up after him? As if....

No, not after him. Not for him. With him. Did you think that might work...

Yes. We followed each other. New York, Trivandrum... That was important. We could...

What?

Mmm...

What?

Hang on!

Skye paused.

Understand one another, she said. Takes time. And it helps.

Nia returned. Go on, she said. I want to listen.

Skye sipped her coffee.

I remember the nights in Bud's. Not weekends, they were full on. We'd be downstairs, I'd be looking for shots, Carp would be just... sucking it all up. For his writing. Together with the booze and the smoke at the back door. That's where the topers congregated and the police just let them be...

You don't do that now...

No. Don't need it. But a good cabernet's different. That Bulgarian is fine with me. So, weekend nights were a sort of coma. But, Mondays, Tuesdays we recovered. I'd wake up and hear the ice groans from the river.

Eh?

It wasn't far away, the South Saskatchewan. Serious river. I mean, a real real river.

Okay.

And from November this real real river froze over, so there was only a narrow channel. That ice was scary the first time you heard it. Like an animal in the dark.

24

Some days I'd go down to look at that ice. Like marrow-bone, the colour of that ice. Watch the anglers trying for mooneye, casting into the unfrozen channel.

By March the ice was thick, the floes grinding against each other. Like river icebergs. No, a river glacier, that ice. And mornings, sometimes a hoarfrost, blue in the car headlights, the Manchurian elms outside another kind of blue.

Your trees?

You bet. Those trees were like ghosts. And the frost was another layer over the ice... Oh, how's Ffrez?

Getting up. She's fine. Go on.

Engrossed, isn't she? And boy, I'd wake up. Tuesday was the best night, the traffic past Bud's long gone, and I'd just...

Yeah?

Listen to the ice's language. I trained myself to wake. That language was so strange. Sad. No, grievous. It was like some-body alive grieving for, what...? Loss? Life itself.

Yes.

And the first time I heard it I came to realize Carp was awake too. And listening to the ice.

That's nice.

Yeah?

Course!

Awake like me. With me. But a stranger in my bed. As I was a stranger in his bed. The smokers had vanished from the back door, the jamming finished. And here I was, listening to a river. Listening to a river that came out of the fucking Rockies, came out of the prairies, came into my head, came into my ear in a room above a blues club. A bar that stank of white widow.

Oh, that's strong. Hard core, weren't you?

No! But Christ, I used to think, how did I get here? I'd be shaking, but not from the cold. Shaking in, what? Excitement? No, not that. Yeah, expectation. And I'd realize that Carp was shaking too. Trembling for the same reason. I never asked him, but yes, that's what I thought. Being alive together...

Like we are now?

Together.

You're lucky, said Nia. You've travelled. You've been places.

Hey, we're going somewhere this week where nobody's ever been. Remember that.

I am, I am.

Look, I remember once coming into Bud's after a walk to the ice. Down by the bridge, those mooneye fishermen stamping in the cold. The frost was smoking, like the waves at The Horns. Our spindrift smoke. And the landlady came up to me with this jar. 'Hey honey,' she said, 'why don't you try this?'

Ooh, hey honey. Hey honey, mimicked Nia.

Why weren't you ever an actress? laughed Skye. Anyway, it was saskatoonberry jam and she'd picked the saskatoonberries herself. Boy, you couldn't have imagined anyone more unlike your typical jam-maker. No Jerusalem with that mother. Now, she was hard core!

Yeah?

You bet. She sometimes sang blues herself, plinking barrelhouse. Yeah, hard-looking woman. Irongrey hair. Leather waistcoat even. But she polished that butcherblock bar in Bud's on her ownsome. Said nobody else could get it to shine like she did.

Cleaned the restrooms too when her old man rebelled. Broken mirrors, miscarriages, the lot. Stayed up with a glass of Wheatland Rye… That's how I really got to know her, closing time at Bud's. Interesting group she allowed to stay behind.

Always loved a lock-in, said Nia. Well, the theory of it…. I'm a landlady too, remember.

We both are.

We call time just when we want…

That's power.

The two women clinked coffee cups.

Well, there was this writer, Carpenter got friendly with… Big John. Marooned on the prairie. Used to smuggle in a pint of Bushmill's. I was always expecting Jeanne to find out, but maybe they had an arrangement. His Irish, her Sask.

Sounds a great place.

Because we were all like that, I realized. People who'd discovered a sanctuary. Daresay there's a new gang nowadays. Not sure about Big John, though. Carp was going to ask him down to Amsterdam Avenue. Three days on a Grey Goose. To do readings together. Never worked out. But Jeanne's still there, I've heard.

Quite a scene.

Like we're doing, love.

Like Parry tried, with *Badfinger*…

Yeah, Parry tried.

Anyway, Jeanne talked about growing up on a prairie farm. That farm, she said, included a big soda lake. Never froze, that soda, even when it was fifty below. Not a fish. Dead, see.

Dead Sea?

Oh yes. Kind of. Couldn't swim in it. Didn't have a name either, she said. So even the Cree hadn't bothered.

Cree?

Woodland Cree. Local injuns. Christ, over here that lake would be famous. Jeanne had been with the Angels before taking on Bud's but got tired of boring bikers... She was hilarious about bikers. So she walked away. And they let her. Respect, see... Respect.

Gotta walk away some time, said Nia.

Like we will. Anyway, thanks, I said. Thanks, Jeanne. And you know? That was good jam! Carp had it on toast. Hey, we should pick blackberries, by the way. This weather's bringing them on early.

What are they like?

What?

Those berries?

Saskatoons? There was a tree behind Bud's. Carp used to bounce a ball against it, when he was thinking about a story. Green unripe, then kind of red, then kinda black. Succulent, not too sweet. Maybe Jeanne had picked berries off that same tree...

Fancy her...?

That tough titty? No way. Jesus. You're my type.

If you have a type. Have I seen a photo?

There are some, yeah. Jeanne at her famous bar, or the piano. The artists I usually shot in the dressing room. That dungeon under the stage.

Get them out, when we're back.

You've seen one set.

Yes?

That's the trouble with photographs. Nobody remembers.

I remember. Now.

But, Bud's Blues Club. Benzedrine's glamour and squalor, that's what I was aiming for. And Carp too, with his prairie stories.

Like to read one.

Which were good. Title of his collection was going to link *prayers* and *prairie*. *The Wolverine* was another possible. Not so real to me because he swore he'd never seen one. A wolverine, I mean. Only he'd once been to Wolverine Street up in Banff. Yeah, Carp had travelled all over. But that bar was important to both of us.

An older child at the toy table bumped Ffresni over. Nia went across and righted her daughter. But Ffrez's outrage was shortlived.

And Carp liked all that? suggested Nia coming back.

He loved the space over there. Me? I found it scary at first. Like living without history. But he and Big John joined this group, *Illegal Jazz Poets* they called themselves and did a couple of sets... Carp looked forward to those gigs. Had to dose himself with the iceberg vodka, but...

See! Hard core, weren't you?

Nothing like, love. We wanted jam, remember. On English muffins. And brunch, they were big on brunch over there. Hash browns? Eggs Benedict? Great for spaced out, coming down Sunday mornings...

Strung out?

No, we weren't like that. We worked! Okay, had a few puffs at the back door but Jeanne wouldn't have allowed much else. Well, lemon haze, I recall that.

Sounds nice. Anything else?

Okay, skunk.

Nia raised an eye.

But not super skunk! That was forbidden by Jeanne, and Brad, her partner. You should have seen his gear under the counter.

My cudgel, remember. Still got it.

Well, Brad was an ice hockey player, one of the enforcers for the Blades... Ever felt a hockey puck?

Don't tell me he was a jazz poet!

Er, no. So Carp kept his distance, I suppose. But we all tolerated one another. I saw how Bud's worked, the mechanics of it. What it needed. A ton of work.

Here's a ton of work!

It is! Yeah, take yourself seriously! That's what Jeanne taught me. But I knew already of course. Work is prayer. Who said that?

You did.

I mean first.

The fucking Nazis, laughed Nia. You told me that once.

No, they had *Work Sets you Free*...

Yeah?

In iron writing on the Auschwitz gates.

Well that doesn't sound...*wrong*.

It's not *wrong*. But the way they meant it was wrong.

You been there too? asked Nia.

I'll get the shots out for you...

See. Everywhere.

Black and white. In the snow.

See.

And you can judge if they're clichéd. Think I rushed them. Sort of generic. Polish snow, black rails going nowhere. White sky...

See.

Travel isn't everything.

Everywhere. Lucky cow.

Just different circumstances.

But I'm really starting to think that I missed out.

Look, said Skye, nowhere is better than this. That's what you learn, chicken.

IV

Ike walked around the shop. In one corner Serene was sorting packets of bamboo socks, down on one knee, the other knee pointing towards him.

In black tights, he noticed. Maybe a purple seam. He looked and looked away and Serene looked away. Ike thought she was going to say something, but didn't.

Yes, usually quiet, this one. At least when he was around. Then he looked at the girl again.

Are we all ready? he asked finally.

Serene straightened.

Yes. Lois is in the back room.

Come on then...

Children take time, she said. You're not used to it...

He looked at her again. Oval face, fine as bone china. Interesting hair. Something classical about her. Whatever that meant.

They take so long, he said.

Tell any parent...

But you're not... So how do you know?

She looked at him again. And shook her head.

★

Millions of gallons a day, said Nia. And that's not to mention the other resurgences. But where does the water come from?

Some of it river water leakage, said Ike. Some of it spring water. Vexes the experts.

Hey, I love that word, said Nia. Vex!

So I'm not ashamed to say, continued Ike, that... I'm not sure...

Hallelujah, said Nia. Magic water. Or, water is magic.

I just like the mystery, said Skye. Please don't explain.

We all have to know about this, said Ike. Life and death... You know that, Skye.

Of course. I'm taking it seriously. Yes! But I want photographs of somewhere that's never been shot before. We all know safety's vital.

What I meant, said Nia, was that there's enough water. That's for sure. Six million gallons every day usually? And still a lot even in this dry time. That's what I thought when I was in the caving club at college. There's a world we don't see. And it's real. Supporting us. We'd be nothing without it.

They'd reached the new harbour. Serene was ahead holding Ffresni's hand. The pair were finishing a peanut-butter-flavoured ice cream Ike had bought in the fairground. Extra-crunch.

Below on the boardwalk of the jetty a party of anglers was unloading their catch. Already they had the harbour scales outside, plus a measuring tape. Two of the party were holding an enormous fish between them. One of them in waders was putting something in the fish's mouth.

Think... said Ike. Shark. No wait, I'm wrong. That's a... That's a *conger*. Jesus Christ.

They moved down steps to the new quay. Nia told Serene not to bring Ffrez near.

Where'd you catch that? asked Ike.

One of the men looked up. Spat. He was adjusting the cigar he'd positioned in the eel's mouth.

On the reef. Been fishing there thirty years.

Well known, said Ike. Perfect for eels.

Tell us about it, said the fisherman. I've been hearing people talk all my life about one like this. In the end we reeled it in. So far. Then I stopped the boat and we walked it in. Walked it in, I tell you. Top of the reef. Above sea level! It was out of the water, the slimy bastard. Unreal.

I've been over there once, said Ike. There's that lagoon. And the ship's boiler, you can see it from shore. When the sun's on it. Copper, I think. And those caves…

Lot more besides, said the man. My son's a diver and says it's a maze of tunnels under the reef. All unmapped. Perfect for eels. Too narrow for a man…

What about a woman? asked Skye.

Welcome to it, love. Need to be a skinny piece. No turning round. Once you're in you're in.

He and the other angler now had the conger gaffed and chain-hung. Seen this way it was bigger. Maybe ten feet long.

Look at this cunt. Might be forty years old, Teg says. He's over in the office now…

Surprising, said Ike.

The man paused. Gave me a fuckin surprise, I can tell you. We got the daddy here. We got the king. Well, the queen. I'll open its mouth for you. Don't worry, we've finished it off. Can lose fingers, see. Blokes I've known. Or hands.

Smooth, isn't it, said Nia.

Look at those teeth. Jam it open, I will. Jaws on that? Like a cobra. Dislocates, see. Dislocates itself. My son's bringing the other camera. Should be here by now... Be in the papers, this will... This is the daddy.

Maybe female, said Skye.

Well, yeah. This is female. So big, see. Big ones are always...

Yes, said Nia. I've heard the stories... But never thought... Ooh, look at those teeth...

Like the limestone on the reef, said Ike. Daggers.

Just when we copped on, said the fisherman, Teg was talking about the weever fish that's around now. Hot weather, see. Now, they can nip. But nothing like this thing might.

Nia had noted the number of anglers in the town. Yes, it was the extraordinary weather, she thought. And remembered John Vine talking about garfish. Those green garfish on a barbecue near The Horns. Sucking a green bone. Caught in the eelgrass, John Vine had said.

What'll you do? asked Ike.

Sell it. There's no fishmonger around here with a slab big enough. And the scales is too small here. So, try the supermarket boys. Not that eel is popular. Nobody wants eel. Ever bought eel in a restaurant? Would you eat that thing?

Why d'you catch it then? asked Nia.

The fisherman ignored her. Don't worry. It'll go somewhere. They'll cut it. Some kind of fish stew. French name. So we have to take pictures.

The man had put his balled fist into the eel's mouth. Charcoal-grey, that eel. Cold as a lid of ice on a dune slack. Cold as water from The Shwyl. Blood had run out of the conger's mouth. There was a pool of blood on the new boardwalk.

With her forefinger Nia traced the eel's skin pattern. There was a glistening brown mixed into the grey and black. Its belly was paler, dingy yellow. Or like bark, she thought. Bark of a young tree. More intricate, that pattern the closer she looked into it. Infinite, she thought.

Wish I'd had my bolster, said the angler. Just sharpened it on the grindstone. Could have done with it on the reef.

Something...*mythological* about this, whispered Skye.

Supermarket? asked Nia. Get an eel in the fist and that's money.

Fist? asked the fisherman. This could have taken my arm off. Still counting fingers.

I mean money's hard to keep hold of. Like an eel. But this is an enormous eel. Like nothing I've ever seen.

Fuckin right, it's big. Maybe the biggest. But it was always there. Waiting. It'll be a YouTube, the boy'll see to that. Be all over Facebook. Filmed it, see. Till it got a bit hairy. We needed every hand free...

The man considered.

Teg's got a lump hammer he uses for sharks. Fuckin four pounder. Lovely heft. Or fathead, even. Ever seen a real fathead? That's cod to you.

I know, said Nia.

That one the hurricane blew on to the golf course. See that? Showed people how big cod can get. That was on telly.

I was away travelling then, said Ike.

Thornbacks can get biggish, the man continued. Smooth-hound the same. Course, that's your small shark. Sea's full of small sharks. Small sharks trying to be big sharks.

But this isn't a shark, said Skye.

Dogfish get big. But never like this. Wait till they see the film in the pub…George'll put it up on screen. Framed picture of me and the boys too. With that thing. I'll make sure of that.

How far you think those tunnels go? asked Ike.

No knowing, is there. Reef seems to be a real mess of gwlis. It's a maze down there. Christ, where's that fuckin camera…

Wouldn't want to come face to face with this, said Nia.

Give you a kiss, love. Pucker up. Nah, they're more scared of you. That's what people say, anyway.

Well… said Nia.

But you're right. Not for me either, love. Wouldn't fancy it at all. Too many corners for me, down in the coldwater coral. I'd rather go shopping than dive under that reef.

You get used to it, said Ike.

The man lifted an eyebrow.

Well, Teg better be back really soon. Or this fucker will have smoked his cigar.

V

They went as far as the second moraine. Skye was using one of the caving torches, but Serene ignored the beam. She climbed down the pebbles filling her sack with sticks: spills for kindling, spars and splinters for the heart of the fire.

When she had taken three loads to camp she returned with a bough. This had been bleached to ivory after years afloat.

Always great for drift, this place, she said. Nia's right. I've been three times now and it's perfect.

Yeah, said Ike Pretty. The best. Better than Caib cliffs. Much better than The Horns.

Yeah?

Oh yes. I'm a driftwood connoisseur, me. The currents here catch it right.

But what are you like lighting fires?

We're using matches? Then one match. Bet you.

Yes?

Certain. Let me do the kindling...

Ike began to sort through the stack.

What about this, he said. In no particular order we have saltwort root, tarry rope, piece of blackboard, more tarry rope. Which could burn. Make a great wick. Yeah, this could burn all night. Be burning tomorrow... I love how driftwood burns. So clean.

Ever been in The Chasm? asked Serene.

Dived there, said Pretty. Much deeper than people think.

Maybe one hundred feet. No kidding. Last summer, no equipment, nothing. Down as long as I could manage.

There'll be no diving in The Shwyl, said Skye, also organising the pyre. Nia's terrified by the idea.

Look, said Ike. We're not taking diving kit down. Okay, masks, but no cylinders. Can't lug those. I might scope it out…

Mask for me too, said Skye. Course. If it's good enough for Prettyboy here…

So, you been down The Chasm, said Serene. Where else you travelled?

Name it. Last place was Libya, before the trouble. There's a meteorite field I camped on. Weird place. Like the moon might be. I brought one home.

One what home?

A meteorite.

Yeah?

Yeah.

How?

It's here.

Ike indicated the thong around his neck. Just a fragment of iron, he said. I like the idea it might have come from a different system.

System?

Different solar system. Around a different sun.

Let's see.

Ike revealed the nugget on its leather cord.

Somebody told me it was probably radioactive, he said.

What about underground?

Anywhere in limestone. Look at a map. The US sometimes. And not far from here... Caverns becoming caves becoming... passageways. Sometimes a squeeze, sometimes a sump... You never know.

Gives me the creeps, laughed Serene. No, really... Some of your photographs! Ugh. That one in Arizona... Looks like you were completely stuck... How'd you get out?

I think myself thin.

Well you look like a caver. Kind of skinny. Is *wiry* a word?

If you like.

And Nia's getting trim.

Doesn't she look great? She'll have no troubles. After all, this is her idea...

I think she's scared...

Don't be stupid, said Skye. Just worried about leaving Ffresni a few hours... And look, we had words because I collected some of those stones she brings off the dunes.

Yes, I heard those words, laughed Serene.

The corals? They're fine in the shop, but they've spread to the bedroom... All I said was take pictures, not samples... Christ, I sat on an ammonite in the bath...

VI

Bowels of the fire.

Bonegrey driftwood.

Dead of night.

*

The fire threw shadows over the sand. Ike walked into the firelight.

Hey, said Skye. Like the shoes.

He looked down. Only ones to hand, he said. Steelies from Goodyear.

Yeah, nice. Are they red?

Yes.

Man in the red shoes. There's fancy...

Skye laid a spar across the fire.

But Isaac Pretty, she said slowly, you're a fantasist.

It's on my website.

And the Net never lies? asked Nia.

Look, this Johnny Tarr? He's your nemesis, said Skye.

How?

He's always ahead of you. Climbs, caves?

Caves, yes. Climbs? Well...

Girls?

Johnny Tarr's gay.

Liar.

Could be.

You're jealous.

All right, how would I know? admitted Isaac Pretty. But he's seven years older than me...

Not that you're counting...

And had the breaks. Have to get the breaks... You know that. Comes from a climbing family. Was brought up to it. Born on the end of a rope, he always says.

They all say that.

No, that's his famous quote.

It's generic! They all say that. Cliché!

Look, my father...

Dai Pretty?

Yeah. He loved rugby, played guitar with mates...

Fflint and that lot?

Yeah. So it was a miracle I went to college. Dad couldn't see the point. Wanted me to get a job in that dry cleaning business on Caib Street.

Never?

Handy, he said. Local. You won't need to travel. They're even expanding into carpets, he promised. Those shampooing machines. It's the future, he said. Know what our shop was called?

Think I know...

Yeah. *Easy Street.* Jesus, Dad, I thought. So he worked there. For years. If only... But that's what people did. They stayed put. Here. But you and me, we got out...

But we came back.

For a good reason, kiddo.

Sure about that?

Couldn't resist your offer.

Generous, aren't we?

So we're all sure. Aren't we? asked Ike.

Think so.

★

Now Isaac Pretty scooped away sand for his shoulder and then for his hip. But he didn't lie down. Instead he threw another driftwood knuckle on the fire. Then a spar, after cracking it in half. He could smell the salt in the wood. Sea pollen, Nia called it.

Some people, he said, referred to the work as demolition. Others, the scrap business. Yeah, I was a scrappie. A *tatterman*. But big things. Enormous. Once I worked on an aeroplane. All that insulation, all that plastic. Up in smoke. Incredible. Couldn't do it now...

No, said a muffled voice in the dark. It might have been a question.

And a ship once, not far from here. Maybe one thousand tonnes, that ship. Where those scrapyards go down to the sands. Orchard Levels they call it. And we were taking that ship apart. Four of us unscrewing, unbolting. Unriveting when we could. Boy, the size of those wrenches we were using. But if the rivets had seized we'd cut.

And two, just two, with cutting gear. I loved the lance they taught me to use. Yeah, that oxyacetylene lance, its flame from yellow to invisible. That was when it was hottest. Could slice a man in half and no-one would know.

Yes, hottest when it cut through the thousand metal bits we needed to…dismantle. Down in the hold in the dark. It was a cave in there. Dripping, dank. A real cave, that hold.

He paused, as if waiting a response. None came.

Then I'd climb below the hold. Bilge sludge under my feet. Thick on the walls. Oh yeah, the cave under the cave.

Journey to the centre of the earth, muttered Skye in the firelight.

Those taps and pumps, we cut them all out. And just the four of us taking a ship apart. That oxy smell in my hair and clothes. And always in the air. Never got rid of it.

He looked into the firelight.

Sometimes it was just me. Down there, I mean. Weird shadows but mainly pitch dark. And my own shadow in the spotlights. Just him and me. Like in this firelight.

Again he paused, brushing away sand hoppers.

And echoes. All this echoing. You know that hollow sound at the bottom of a ship? Sometimes I slept there to save money and time. Used to fall into my blankets, big suck of whisky, and it would be morning. Time to start all over again. With another slug if I could stomach it. I was at it by four. No, five most days. Because sometimes I had two sucks of that Jura. Yeah, if not a decent rum, always Jura. Thought it tasted of peatwater. And hot as hell, burn of a burn. Kept me alive.

Like we're doing now, said Skye, passing on the hipflask.

And music in the bilge. Deep under the deck with a stack of old cassettes tapes. Ever hear the MC5? Hey, anyone? Out there?

No, said Skye's voice.

Discovered the MC5 from this bloke who was with me on the oxy. Used to turn the tape to max and play one song over and over. *Kick out the Jams, Motherfuckers.* Heard it?

No, said Skye. Thank God.

Mad music. Madmen's music. Just us down in the dark. In the bilge. Spotlights like I say giving these shadows and that song echoing off the metal walls. And me and this real head-case, this real motherfucker, screaming down there in the dark.

My idea of hell, whispered Skye.

He was older than me. Sinbad they called him. He was a punk rocker, no, a real one, knocking on a bit, yeah, but his hair was still dyed kinda red... Yeah, Sinbad. He was earning a fortune, must have been. Told me I was lucky to be working with him. Learning off him. Now I know that was true.

Nia lay another driftwood branch on the fire. In the darkness to the south she could hear a curlew. What's that smell? she whispered.

Jellyfish, said Ike. Came in on the last high tide. Stinking now.

The three around the campfire breathed in. Hundreds, said Skye. Maybe more.

You know, murmured Ike, sometimes it felt like we were a mile underwater. Just me and Sinbad. Us and the MC5.

I wonder why, said Skye behind the blaze.

Yeah, that Fred Sonic Smith, now there was a guitarist. Greatest recording studio ever, that hold. Fred would have loved it. His godalmighty racket bouncing off the bulkhead. Died of cancer, didn't he?

Shame, said Skye again from the dark

Once, Sinbad and I went to the Red House. Think it's closed now. The Red House?

No idea, said Skye.

Now Sinbad, he took his work seriously. But every now and then he'd fancy a break from routine. And Christ, you should have seen what he could put away. Got into an argument about music in the pub. Didn't like it, did he? Other people's bad music in public. Thought it said something about a man. Badge of honour. Like your soul was on display.

Probably got an iPod now, eh? murmured Skye. Or tuned into Spotify.

If he's still with us. But MC5? That says it all about Sinbad's taste. Not a man to cross.

Obviously.

Glaswegian. Came from a place called Auchenshuggle. He spelled it for me. Born on the day the last tram ran. Never understood a word he said...

You were probably deaf.

Yeah. That was Sinbad. Piercings all over his face. His fish hooks he called them.

Takes all sorts.

Big S tattooed on his forrid. That tells you something. But just us with those lances. Cut you in half, those burning bars.

Their invisible flames.

Charming, said Nia. What's the word?

Catharsis? said Skye.

Don't knock it, said Ike Pretty. Had to be done. I'd never used oxy before. Got the scars to prove it. Christ, we broke every rule. And one rivet at a time, remember. That's when I got used to masks and breathing through tubes. How I learned not to be scared of the dark. And if you'd been in the bilge for two months with Sinbad you...

Sounds like a prison term, said Skye.

As I say, I learned. Never stopped. Then later, it turns out I'm in a cave in Palawan, just looking, only looking, and the guide, a local kid, points out the flying foxes roosting in the roof.

Foxes? said Nia from the dark.

Kind of bat. Big buggers, those flying foxes. Very big. Wings like funeral crepe.

Won't be any in...

No, course not. Might be bats, though. That's normal for caves. Thick as soot, bats. And think of their shit. Thousands of years of batshit. But it all came back to me in that cave in the Philippines. You see, the ship was called *The Flying Fox*. Sinbad's ship. Don't know why. Strange name for a ship, but it made me think...

About? asked Skye.

About how everything comes back, said Ike slowly. No matter how far it travels. Look, here's me, back on The Caib. After I swore it wouldn't happen...

But you had to go first? asked Nia. Didn't you? And now you've been everywhere...

That's why you're invited, said Skye. We feel we're in good hands...

VII

Nia leaned a pallet into the fire. She had found it herself on the moraine, dragging it through the sand.

And what about you then? asked Ike. It was dark but obvious he had Skye in mind. You know…life before *Extraordinaria*?

Skye was settled in shadow beside the driftwood. Like the others, she had scooped a hollow in the sand.

Well, me and Carp…

Carpenter? asked Ike. That bloke you were going….

Carpenter, yes. And yes, we were together. For a while.

Writer, wasn't he?

Still is, I suppose. He won't stop that. As he always said, what else can he do?

What about something useful?

Like buggering about in caves? Listen, none of us does anything useful. Except Nia. She's keeping the high street respectable. My heroine. And love, listen, Ffrez is fine. Lois is superb with her. We'll see her in a few hours.

Nia muttered in the darkness.

Canadian? asked Ike at the fire's edge.

For his sins. Island off Vancouver. Moved to the prairies because property was so cheap. You could buy whole towns not so long ago. I went with him to places that existed on the map, but boy, there was little evidence they were ever there. Maybe a grain elevator…

So what did he write?

Journalism. Short stories. Had a story in the *New Yorker*.

Great...

But one only. That's the problem with writers. Always on the next project. Moving away from something that works...

To something that doesn't, said Ike. Not only writers. Bloody Sinbad was the same. Want something dismantled? Sinbad would do it. Always moving on. Christ, I did it for a while...

Course, said Nia from the other side of the fire. We all do it. Have to.

Hey, hissed Skye. Whose story is this? I met Carp in Saskatchewan. I was photographing those vanished towns. You know, Cadillacs with dogwood growing through the floor. Found a great Fleetwood once... Big fins. Like the Cadillac red fin. Abandoned canola farms...

What's canola? asked Ike through the fire.

Rape, honey. Yeah, I prefer rape. More shocking. As it should be.

But... breathed Nia. Rape's a horrible word.

Well, yes, said Skye. It's pretty bad, I suppose.

No, said Nia again. It's the very worst word.

Canola's not so great, laughed Ike.

Nia was invisible behind the fire. Skye continued speaking.

Suppose Carp was writing about this Ukrainian town lost in the prairie... Totally abandoned. Bumped into him in the churchyard there. This onion-domed church stuck out in absolute nowhere. We met at a graveside...

Romantic, laughed Ike.

Don't stir. But it was. In a way. I was photographing what remained of the town. And Carp was writing something…

Did he ever finish it?

Who knows? He always said, and I can hear him now, nothing's ever finished. Everything's a work in progress. Including you. Us. *Abandoned* is a better word… But it energised his soul, I'll say that. Made his mind move. Which is what everybody wants.

Too true, said Nia.

And that's why…

Why what?

Why we got together. And I'll never forget that headstone. Seven children. Pioneers, they called them. These seven Ukrainian children, these pioneer children, burned together one afternoon. Or, a better word, a word Carp used. *Consumed*, he wrote. He showed it to me in his notebook. *Consumed one afternoon.* There was no firebreak, you see…

Maybe, said Ike quietly, it was just that word brought you close.

Isaac Pretty said the word to himself. Then repeated it.

Consumed.

Nia repeated it across the fire.

Consumed.

Could have been, muttered Skye. Who knows? And then we went into the church. Together. Doing something together. For the first time.

Yeah, romantic…

And you know, those graves were kept better than that abandoned church. The vestments were still hanging there. On a rack of webs. And the altar with its chalices? It was mantled in pigeon shit. Yes, that's another word Carp used. He wrote 'the altar arraigned with its chalices'. I remember that too. *Arraigned*. From the same notebook. Little black hardback from Sears. But quite classy. Don't know if he actually used the word in anything finally printed. But in that church there was a statue of Christ, and an albino Christ, I'm telling you. A Christ fiery with lime, outstretched behind the altar. In that abandoned church. Miles from anywhere.

In the darkness a curlew's voice repeated. Nia pulled sand hoppers out of her hair.

But to cut a very long story short, we both drove back to town. Took us the rest of the day. And yeah, it's coming back, what Carpenter had written in his notebook. He described a dead porcupine. Just roadkill, but kind of tragic. Tragic to me, that is. I saw three on that same trip. *Roadkill Blues* was another of Carp's stories. Think I gave him the title.

Published? asked Ike.

Don't know. Anyway, you know what they call a porcupine? Yeah?

Old man of the willow… I'll never forget that. This little face under its warbonnet.

Old Man of the willow? said Ike from his side of the fire. That works…

Think it's native. Woodland Cree, maybe, according to Carp's notebook. Well, Carpenter, he was staying with a university friend. I was lodging at a seminary. Which was brave of those old monks. We rendezvou'd at the only bar on Temperance Street. Or, maybe it was the first bar to be opened. In fact, I remember a campaign to stop a topless club starting up there...

You won, didn't you? asked Nia.

Sort of. But the whole city was just reacting to pressure coming north, coming out of the Net. Kind of unstoppable.

So, you're in this temperance bar, said Ike.

This was a real bar. Honey. We decided to extend our visits through the winter. The snow stayed on the ground for six months. By then it was khaki-coloured. So, we moved into a rented apartment. Above a blues club, I kid you not. Got a monthly deal...and it worked, after we learned to live with the twelve bar jamming...

Not bad, said Ike.

Turned it into joint projects. I took photographs of the performers and the clientele. Some of those fans drove unbelievable distances. Six hours one way. Sometimes starting where there were no roads. Ever heard of towns like La Ronge? Superb?

Course, said Ike. He seemed to be laughing. But not much temperance in a blues club, he added.

Too true. Look, vodka was our poison. There was this real clean brew. Made from water drawn off melting icebergs. Or so they claimed. At least climate change is good for one thing, Carp always said. Got turned on to it in Bud's. That was the name of the club.

So? Ike asked through the fire. He threw on more pieces of drift, creating bushels of sparks.

So, I took some of my best shots. Ever. These black guys out of Chicago or Harlem even, marooned for a night on the prairie. Or black chicks getting off a forty hour Grey Goose and going back after their gig. Jesus, so many of those acts had no idea where they were... Just sent by their agents into the interior. Think John Lee Hooker had been there once. Before our time.

Wow, muttered Ike. Love Hooker. What about Sonny Boy Williamson?

Don't know. But usually I had them pose on the empty stage. Against the empty bar. Or sometimes the dressing room. But the bar, usually. Bit like our empty province. Meanwhile, well...

Carpenter was writing his stories, suggested Ike.

Course he was. I know he tried some things about Bud's but the *New Yorker* didn't like them. Well, they sat on one in particular. Which wasn't fair. Stopped Carp offering it elsewhere. But they must have been considering it. Probably still are. Editor's options, if you understand me...

Where the power resides, said Isaac Pretty.

But I loved that apartment. Our window looked across two streets. We were next door to a theatre so there were always plenty of people. With Manchurian elms outside, autumn leaves a deep orange.

You don't expect Fall on the prairie but that tree was special... Leaves like lanterns and with the sun behind it each leaf was like a lighthouse pane... And my face up there in that burning tree.

You know, I've thought of going there myself, said Ike through the fire's shadows. But the geology's all wrong...

Blame God, hissed Skye. Yeah, Canadian Shield. It's big enough. But what a club, Bud's was. Kind of a refuge for the local misfits. And they weren't all blues aficionados. Hippies, punks like your Sinbad. Farm wives going stir crazy. Even some of the Cree out of the Barry Hotel... Yeah, and this band, the *Illegal Jazz Poets*. All kinds of desperation. Carpenter started a novel there. Writing on a broken saloon table ringed by coffee mugs... Boy, we were coffee junkies in that apartment... Well, the rate he worked, he might be finishing it pretty soon... Rewrite after rewrite, just chucked...

And you took photographs, said Ike, throwing on a length of rope. He examined the sparks in its frayed end.

I made sets, agreed Skye. Like chapters in a book. Great shots of this young guitarist down from Loon Lake. Lived in the bible bashers' camp there. Now that was remote.

Lot of that? asked Ike.

Not heavy. Carp and I thought, suppose like other people, about hiding away in the province. It's kind of undiscovered.

And huge, said Ike.

But there are survivalists, I think they're called... As well as people waiting for the Rapture...

What about the cold?

Oh yes, we were fanciful. Some of those farm wives were getting desperate for lack of...

Can imagine, said Ike.

But what a little star, the axekid. He had the look, know what I mean? *The look.* Might have been trans. Bit of Bolan. Bit of Bowie… Expect he was. Is. Beautiful kid.

There was a boy like that two years ahead in school, said Nia.

Yeah, remember Florence? laughed Ike.

Shut up, said Skye. This kid was like that shitty Christ in the Ukrainian church. Which was beautiful too. Got those shots stashed somewhere, all part of the archive. And I told Carp not to get rid of his drafts, but he didn't see the point…

You should have saved them for him, said Ike. Dutiful girl-friend and all…

As if! But I didn't believe the kid's parents liked what I did. Sixteen when I filmed him. And who knows where he is now.

Got a good idea, said Ike.

Boy, he could play… Lefthanded cat. But what I think now is…what in hell did he know? About the blues? I mean, the fucking *blues*…?

There was a silence. In the darkness they could hear the curlew on the estuary, waves breaking far out on the reef. Nia rose and placed three more spars crosswise in the fire and added her own piece of tarry rope.

VIII

The three around the fire rose to stretch their legs before settling back down.

Your turn, Nia, said Ike.

There was silence.

Can't think, Nia said eventually.

Go on.

Mind's blank. Gotta sleep.

We're all joining in, said Skye out of the darkness. Though Serene is snoring.

The fire was lower, there were hollows in its honeycomb.

We know you're tired.

Nia felt a tear form and run down her cheek. Ffresni in the darkness was what she saw. Her daughter in absolute dark. Where nothing had existed and no word had been spoken or heard. Ffrez in unseeable dark.

Why the hell had she agreed to... But what had she agreed...?

If Nia closed her eyes and waited she could glimpse her own eyelids. Maybe a glimmer of red. A suggestion of her own blood or the womb where the child had grown. She thought she saw the redness of that blood because that's what blood would become. Blackness. A black enameling. Glittering until it dulled to dust. Her own blood. Black mould in a cave, a cave where no light had ever shone. There were places such as that. She was preparing to visit one.

But when had she ever glimpsed such darkness? Nia recalled a girl with black hair she had been with in school. It shone like new tar, that hair. Bubbling in a tar kettle.

She could see the girl in the showers, ringing out the rope of that hair, pretending to whip the girl next to her. Whipping her with black wire. That black hair against ivory skin. Its droplets shining like earrings.

Or wine, maybe. The cabernets Skye chose for the bar. Their gleam in candlelight when there was something special on. Or in the garden the darkness of aubergine flowers. Blackness, yes, might taste of wine, or of flowers. Maybe there were flowers unknown that grew in The Shwyl.

Yes, and black limestone too, wet against her tongue. Her tongue upon the seep. Limestone was made of lilies, its dust would fill her mouth if she allowed. The oxides of that lodestone. Then darkness would swell inside her if Skye took the wrong turning. If she followed Skye and Isaac Pretty.

But why was she leaving her child? It was insanity. She dug more deeply into the sand, shifting her hip. Nia had been holding a piece of driftwood, fiddling with the blaze. The smoke rose beside her like a figure yet to speak. Above the group the stars were white as the polystyrene that blew out of the waves, a ghost that crept out of the sea.

Yes, go on, mumbled Ike.

But Nia felt she was floating as she looked into the fire. Look at Ike Pretty here tonight, she thought to herself. He'd been snoring in the ash. Too much rum, boyo! she'd thought.

Yes, Isaac Christopher Pretty, caste-marked child of The Caib. An hour previously he'd been trying to surf on a piece of driftwood and disappeared beneath a wave. They'd called but he ignored the women. Because he could. Because he was a fool.

Yes, beautiful Ike Pretty with a Libyan meteorite around his neck and Hindu tattoos on both shoulders. Oh, those baffling gods. The sand and the wind had summoned even that dreamer home.

Ike Pretty? That chancer, that fraud. Was he only three years older than herself? He'd kept himself in shape. Clearly worked on it. Any excuse to show that torso, muscles knotted like iris roots and blue in firelight.

Isaac Pretty? How she'd adored him in school. Ike scaling The Horns of The Caib as if he was not a creature of earth himself, Ike diving into The Chasm and emerging with the starfish he claimed had clung to the cave floor. The same colour as his tattoos, she'd noted.

She'd been there that afternoon and seen how the starfish breathed in his hand, and how Ike's right shoulder under its resplendent god could not stop shivering. The first boy she'd seen with tattoos. Yes, Isaac Pretty, addicted to danger, might have been telling the truth.

Yet they said The Chasm was one hundred feet deep. Impossible, she thought. Inestimable to Nia as was The Shwyl. It was another of his stories, because what was Ike but one of the dreamers who haunted this place, their tales made real by the telling, the same dreams that went round with the carousels, those horses with their emblazoned names, Mary and Madelaine and Nathaniel, stars on their muzzles and all the fairground alive this summer, its population disbelieving as the crowds kept coming. And kept coming.

Day after day they arrived and a new ride had been imported, a hydraulic stem that sent mechanical shoots into the air. High above the town stood that flower, the highest ride there had ever been, a steel sunflower that dwarfed The Ziggurat and the Kingdom of Evil. How they screamed in terror, in delight, the people who came.

Nia was looking into the fire.

Black panther skins. That's what she saw.
In broken sleep while her daughter sang to herself, while the child murmured through the hours before dawn and the shadow of the moon-and-stars mobile played over her bed, she dreamed of snakes. The bodies of black vipers.

These had been brought out by the weeks of hot weather. So much had been encouraged into the open, adders and orchids unseen for years. Orchid blood on the chalk. Adders dark in her delirium.

Her waking dream was of vipers. Two fighting snakes were wrapped around one another, two black vipers with tracings of diamonds on their backs, black diamonds on black snakes. Intent and vicious, those vipers.

Nia!

It was Skye leaning out of the fire towards her.

It's you.

Okay, okay.

Dreamboat.

Sorry.

Yeah, long day.

I was...

What?

Oh nothing...

Your turn?

Okay. Look, it's nothing tropical. All right? Fact is, it's something that happened here. Really close by. See, I haven't got many travellers' tales like you lot.

Don't say that, hissed Skye.

Not a member of the travellers' club, am I?

Who is? laughed Ike. But been there once. Grand place. Go on.

You mean there's a real club?

Oh yes. Regent Street, somewhere like that.

You're joking...

No. Real club. Called 'The Travellers' Club.' Sat in one of the armchairs... Real fire. Bit like this. You could fall asleep. Maybe I did... Lecture about caving in Indonesia. Not bad...

Skye pursed her lips.

So in my story... said Nia.

Yes?

There's no fucking coyotes. Or whatever they were.

They heard Skye inhale.

Okay. It's a campfire story.

Great.

About a real campfire.

Fine.

Is that allowed?

It's allowed.

Nia turned over. Okay, I was here once in spring. The swans had made one of their ridiculous nests, a raft of sticks on the island in the pool. Only it wasn't an island any more. The rains had stopped, the springs, those resurgences, were dry and everything was going back to normal.

She paused after a log spat repeatedly. Nia felt easier because none of them were visible in the darkness. As people said it was on stage, she thought, peering into the blackness.

But this was a human being, I tell you. Oops, sorry, that's the punchline. See, I've never told this story before.

We're listening, said Skye out of the darkness. She seemed to have moved her position.

Sorry. Well, I came around a dune and saw embers, still glowing. There'd been a driftwood fire just like this, branches and pallets brought off the beach, ship's rope. Like now...

Miles of the bloody stuff, said Skye.

Some ships lose it, said Ike. Others cut it.

Much prefer the real rope, said Skye. Not that plastic...

Me too. Love it when ships tie up in the harbour.

Or *Yr Harbwr,* laughed Ike. But that surveillance camera on it? What's that all about? They can watch the sea.

Yes, new cameras all over now, aren't there? said Nia.

But, she continued, have you seen that cruise ship? Restored it. Least it's using the old capstans...

Like boulders, aren't they? said Skye. Ancient.

Part of our heritage...

Knuckles, said Nia. Or...

Thumbs, then? Ike.

Well, both.

Okay, Nia continued. It was a big fire, and there's always driftwood close by. As you know. But also, two swan's wings, broken off, two wings snapped off a swan's body, and lots of swan feathers.

She paused. There was no response.

Long, white and bloody, those feathers, and swan's down, bloody and burned, and swan bones there in the fire. Stripped of the swan flesh. The swan meat. Oh yes, whoever did it was hungry. Or desperate. Determined to get his fill. Swan's bones, gnawed and sucked.

Fox, muttered Ike.

Not a fox, smartarse, they're messy eaters. This was a human being, I tell you.

She halted and once again there was no response.

He, or she... No, he...probably went straight to the nest after stalking the swan and the swan would have challenged him. A mistake, yes. Because some of the people you get over here, it's...it's...

Dangerous? said Skye. It is.

There's all manner of legends. I picked up a swanfeather.

Longer than my arm, white and bloody. A swan up the Swannee...

She seemed to be waiting for a reaction.

Oh, Christ, give us that rum somebody... Maybe I'm not so *diplomatico*....

So... Nia said finally. Okay, that's me done. Serene now... Serene?

But the girl was asleep.

IX

It was Ike Pretty suggested The Cat.

No, Serene complained. I stink of woodsmoke.

Me too, agreed Skye.

Yet somehow they found themselves ordering coffees. Six o clock and already there were tables outside, but they agreed on a remote corner of the bar.

Had enough sunlight for now, said Serene. All I really need is a shower…

And here's me thinking you were hardcore, said Pretty. You know, this is the closest place if you're just off the sand…

He and Skye approached the bar. Despite the early hour, there were several drinkers. Maybe the newcomers were more alert after their night on the dunes. Perhaps those already present were somnolent at that hour. Either way, Skye considered them slow to move.

One man was speaking to George, the bar manager, telling him about sunfish. Several of these had been caught at Caib caves.

They can get bigger than that, said George. Weigh a ton, some of them. Literally. This weather brings them.

Yeah, said Clint, his son. But then, there's lots of weird creatures around now. Aren't there?

A man named Cranc sniggered. There was a pint of lager smoking on the counter before him.

What's funny? asked Skye.

Cranc turned to his left. He sniggered again. Then he turned to face Skye.

What's funny? she repeated. Then faced the bar as if seeking support.

What's funny? said Cranc. You lot. That's what's funny.

He looked for George the barman. But suddenly George wasn't there.

We're funny? asked Skye.

Cranc turned again.

You lot… You lot… he trailed off.

Are funny? queried Skye. Well I don't think we're…*funny*. Do you think we are? *Funny* that it?

She was speaking now to Davy Dumma. Who shook his head. Davy Dumma never spoke. As a rule.

Does anybody else here think that? asked Skye to the bar. That we're, you know, funny?

She took a long look round.

Nobody, eh? she said. Seems it's only you then. Who thinks we're that way. That we're…what's the word…? *Funny?* Is that the word?

Cranc tried to push past. He jolted Skye's shoulder, spilling his own drink. The woman placed her left hand on his arm.

Is that the word?

Cranc struggled against her hold.

Don't go, she said. I want you to tell us, you see. Tell us why we're….

…*Funny*.

As she said the last word her right hand reached down and

gripped Cranc's balls. Skye lifted him so he stood on tiptoe.

What's funny? Tell me. Go on. Give me a clue. What. Is. Funny?

Cranc was making a whining sound. Like air escaping from a radiator.

Go on.

Fff…

Share it with us.

The air continued escaping.

Cranc was prodding Skye's breasts. Two-finger prods as hard as he could manage.

Don't do that, she said.

Cranc continued.

I said don't. Do that.

The prodding went on.

Sky lifted him an inch higher. One of his feet was off the ground.

Cranc summoned the strength for a last attempt at freeing himself.

The woman suddenly released him and he regained the floor. As he did Skye headbutted him to the nose, releasing a bloody jet. Foreseeing its direction, Skye stepped away.

Cranc slumped against the bar as the woman shimmied to the right.

Got a cloth? she asked George who had reappeared. Oh, messy.

Early for trouble, said George. Think it's a record.

X

She felt a grain of sand in her eye. A grain in her broken tooth. Nia looked round at the streambed, pitted and uneven. But it was cooler here. She knelt and pressed her middle finger into the ground. Dry. Utterly.

There was a moon of dirt under her fingernail, she could feel sweat in her groin and the small of her back. But the sand was silk and there was silence in the pit where the water should have risen. But not a breath and not a bubble. No cave breeze.

Then she was pressing her face into the ground. Watermint, she thought, crushed underfoot. But not the freshwater smell she remembered, the swaft of foxpiss and willowsap, that water out of the limestone, its seep from the labyrinth.

Dry again. Good, another week without rain. And tomorrow a dawn without dew.

*

And she waited, listening. Hidden, that cleft under the willows. It had always been her place, hers, even when she had ventured down and found buckled beer cans or energy bottles. No-one might have guessed there was a source there. Or an *emergence*, as she was learning to say. She heard her own breath and beneath that the whine of sap, pitched like mosquito music.

Above her head was a rustle. A bird had come through the canopy and was perched on a branch five feet from her, facing away.

An owl, she saw. Brown, every feather distinct. The colour of sherry, that bird. Hunched, harried that bird. A refugee.

She was not breathing but her heartbeat would surely reveal her presence. So she continued to gaze into the mosaic of its feathers. And the closer she looked the finer the detail that revealed itself...

When she climbed out, Skye had come back. They stood under the willows. Although it was late June the trees were showing first yellow leaves.

Still sleeping?

Fast.

Nia brushed away the perspiration under her nose.

You know, I always went down there to listen to the water. There are three places it comes out. Full spate takes about one week of rain. Then a dry fortnight for the stream to slow. Then to disappear. And then the slacks vanish. As if they were never there.

How's the stream now?

Like it never existed. Dry as ash.

Great.

You know, I used to look at those three places down there.

The resurgences?

Yes, and especially the crater. So clean when it's brimful. And I'd think, those must be some of the tightest squeezes anybody could find.

Honey, those aren't squeezes, said Skye. Nobody could get through there. Crazy for a body to try.

You know what I mean. The passages have to be better where we're going, because...

Course they are...

Or we'll be turning back...

You've seen the entrance, said Skye. We walk in, we don't crawl. All the evidence is that the first squeeze isn't until...

Yes, she's waking. I thought she was.

There was a child slung on Skye's back, wrapped in a red and yellow blanket.

That's a great sleep, said Nia. At last. Now we know what to do. Just bring her over here. The *parraje* never fails. Well, hardly ever...

XI

Business? asked Nia.

Serene smiled and shrugged. Tossed her purple hair.

Over three hundred this morning. While we were gallivanting in the sand.

Yeah, they love Lois, said Skye. Not hard to guess why.

Hot over there now, I'll bet?

Eighty Celsius. Again. And again tomorrow.

Nia looked at the sales ledger.

More bamboo knickers. Why do people buy bamboo knickers in a heat wave. I'll order extra.

They're cool, that's why, laughed Serene. Pricey but cool.

Wear them, do you?

If you can afford to shop here, we're paying you too much, said Skye.

That's why I'm in rags, said the girl, flicking her fringe.

Nia thought about Serene. She was becoming important. Something amusing had recently startled the girl. The explorers had come together before their expedition. Yet they'd been talking about the shop.

But that image became famous, said Nia.

Not really…

Yes it did! Because…

Because of the shape of the wave against the breakwater…

No. Come on, Ni. Because I called it what I called it...

Skye had photographed waves breaking over the lighthouse in one of the hurricanes of the previous year. It was true that people came to the town for this reason in times of bad weather.

Always been known, Ike agreed.

It's worse now.

But good for the town.

Maybe. But all these hurricane-chasers? They come to create clichés.

As all three understood, spectacular waves were guaranteed to occur in local storms at high tides. The images were predictable. Waves had to appear monstrous in relation to the lighthouse. Because of the design of the breakwater where the lighthouse stood these high tide waves did seem enormous.

Photographers arrived from all over the country and abroad in the hope that their lighthouse image might appear on news programmes or front pages. The wave chasers were familiar to locals, and a tiny café had opened, dedicated to the sport. A drink had even been created. Hot chocolate with rum...

Think about it, said Skye. There must be hundreds of pictures of our waves...

No, thousands, said Ike. Shared all over the world.

And I was lucky with the angle I chose.

Lucky? laughed Nia. You're an artist...

No, we all need luck. Right place, right moment. I was on that pub balcony. Just went up there. Didn't ask... Had to pull the blind up...

Great.

When it was developed I thought, yes, that's like, that's like...

A horse's head, said Nia. A horse kind of leaping over the lighthouse...

Well, the horse head nebula. You know, stars...

Which is not really like a horse's head at all, said Ike.

Oh, you sad literalist! said Nia.

What constellation?

Dunno, brainiac!

And I gave the picture a name, said Skye. For once. Don't do that normally, but...

You called it 'horse's head', said Nia.

And that appealed to some editors. And, yes, it was...

Everywhere, said Nia.

OK. And still being used, said Ike. Fair play.

Will be for years, said Nia. A silver horse jumping right over the lighthouse... Like one of our carousel horses... Mary and Madelaine and...

Nathaniel, said Skye.

But what was the name of that hurricane? asked Ike.

Er...Hattie, laughed Skye. I think that also helped. You know, Hurricane Hattie. Alliteration sells.

Sometimes, said Nia. Been some weird names.

Yes, American. But Hattie appealed to editors over here too. Something familiar about Hattie...

So 'horse's head of Hurricane Hattie' couldn't fail. Simple minds, eh?

Made you famous, said Ike, shaking his head. Huge on Twitter and Instagram.

Jealous?

Yeah. No. Well, I am. Was. Could be. But two cheers for Hattie.

When's the next hurricane? asked Nia.

Winter, said Skye. If we get one. Unimaginable isn't it? Sea's like a mirror now… Last night with the moon on it? Incredible. But how could the waves get so angry?

When the tide's out you think it's never coming back… That wave's like the horse's head are out of some fantasy novel. What letter are they on now?

Who can remember in summer? They start again in the next hurricane season. Don't they?

Maybe you should use 'hurricanes' in your own marketing? suggested Ike. After all, everybody's cashing in on climate change now…

Horse's head's in the shop, said Nia. Framed it. We had a few copied.

And they sell, said Skye.

People feel proud, said Nia. Look, this is us. Here's something we're famous for.

So far three copies of Skye's horse's head had sold in *Extraordinaria*. The woman had been encouraged to print images from 'Raccoon Lodge' and 'Bud's' and these were also displayed. No takers yet.

Those black chicks against the bar, she laughed. Think what all of those singers share is a kind of…*bewilderment*. Like, 'how did I get here?' expressions. Or maybe that's just me thinking too much.

Yes, that's you, said Nia. I love those faces. They'd go in the city... But...

It's not about shifting product, is it? said Skye.

Absolutely...

One of Skye's 'Chalai Market' set had sold. And been brought back because it didn't fit a wall. The buyer had been angry and Serene, stunned, had given the money back. She often talked about it.

What the women found was that local artists and photographers were bringing their own images of waves over the breakwater and enquiring about sales. Art was supported by the shop but Nia used lack of wall space as an excuse to reject most work.

Some of these people seem to paint with trowels, Skye once remarked.

That's one technique, Nia answered. Works for some. Pallet knives, hawks and floats. If only they had the talent.

One was still wet, laughed Skye. All that titanium white for the waves. Turner it was not. Thick as cement.

Don't knock the daubers, said Nia.

Someone should paint moonlight on the sea, said Skye. Just as you catch it at the end of Nuestra Senora Street. I'd buy that.

Nothing wrong with a good daub, said Nia. Long as it's not on our walls. But what's the word?

Er...*impasto* I think. But you can take it to extremes. Why not paint with a muck spreader?

Some of them already do, it seems.

I like what you did with that image, said Skye. Putting it through the red filter...

So it looks like a really bloody high tide, said Nia. That's me messing about with your work. But maybe we should put that on the wall. Yeah, 'The Bloody Tide.' It's coming. That might stir someone up...

Too late, darlink, said Skye. Too late.

XII

Skye showered while Nia fed Ffresni, then they both went to their bedroom. It was on the third floor of what had been Clwb y Mor on Cato Street, close to the seafront. Once it had been the Paradise Club. The owners had rewarded Nia by offering her the lease for five years. She and Skye had opened a café and shop in what was the downstairs bar.

Look, said Nia, I've seen those slacks filled by weeks of rain. Later, if there's a wet summer, their surface blue with damsels. Caib Pools we used to call them. I've even walked out on the ice when they were frozen.

Why?

Risk, darling. Why are we going where we're going? Why do those idiots dance on cranes or high ledges? And I've listened to that groan the ice makes. Like something I shouldn't have overheard. Bit like you in Canada.

You'd hardly drown.

They can be ten feet deep, those pools. Last year there were swans and I saw eight. Then realised it was four swans and their reflections. The slacks are like that. Mysterious water. No known source.

That's why we're going...

Two years ago was that wet spring and winter. Constant rain and suddenly a river through the dunes. First time I've ever seen it, following what must be a historic course.

A river remembering where to flow?

Yes. Maybe after a century?And yeah, I thought, water has a memory. Because water's alive...

Right on, girl. Poetry's full of it.Transformations and astonishments. And this water's special.

I know that.

I know you know, smiled Skye.

I know you know I know.Always I went over when the pools were full...

Course...

To watch the waves when the wind blew. Yes, real waves, lapping the dune, those waves breaking against willow. And all that water come from those three resurgences. A word you've taught me.Three craters like three stars, a constellation that shines only when water pours.

That's nice.

Don't be bitchy.

I'm not.

OK. Just thought you'd like it...

XIII

Nia fired the incense stick and turned off the light, then climbed into the bath. It was too full and she thought it might overflow.

Jesus Christ!

Hot.

Too hot.

Jeezuss!

Put up with it, girl.

Oh *Iesu*.

Sit down!

No.

Christ.

Deeper.

Agony.

Scalding!

Past bellyfold.

Up to nipples.

Past mole that might or might not be… Another one on hip. Two on back. Unreachable.

Over breasts. They'd never recover. After Ffrez. Nor arse. Face it. Slackening. Drooperies. Especially arse.

Up to chin.

Up to earlobes. The curls out of the bathing cap wet now.

Over bottom lip. No matter. And no light, not even Cato Street LEDs. No sound. The road silent. Skye had turned her music down. Ffresni sleeping. Maybe an hour. Serene out. At *The Cat.* Maybe new scene. There. Get those girls over. Better here than there. And...

Last of the lavender. Smoke on the water.

Maybe the bath should have been cold. The Shwyl might be wet but not warm. Maybe they should wear oilskins. The gear was waterproof, wasn't it? Maybe she...

Yes, cold. Too bad now. Nia breathed deeply and immersed. Eyes closed. Still she couldn't open her eyes underwater. The Shwyl would taste of limestone. Like the crevices of Caib cliffs. But this water was sweet, its syrup upon her tongue.

Limestone soup, who'd told her that? Serene maybe. The Shwyl would be rank, its air a wet shawl. Wouldn't it? Yeah, Serene's hair's great. Purple again. Black once. Not shining enough then. Bootblack dull but... *aubergine* now. Great colour and not cheap but if you can get away with... Good figure. Those tits. No kids see. Her choice... Still young though.

Nia made herself stay put, feeling the black petals over her eyes and in her throat now. Always the seep, the leaking into. But she had to try. Thorax tight.

She was crying, maybe. Or the air was wet. But tears, tears... Why were tears floating through her head? Could tears float? *Butcher's tears?* What were they? How...

So what had Ike Pretty told her? That story was about…? Yeah, Amsterdam. Never been, have I? Another place… But maybe he'd told Skye too. Maybe he'd told everyone. Last to know, was she? No surprise there, then. No surprises ever.

But that girl he was with. That poor girl. Don't think Ike told us when he met her. Or where. Didn't usually reveal, did he? But, yes, Amsterdam…, that Irish name. *Niamh,* he said. Beautiful. *Niamh,* and so like, so like… That's why Nia had looked it up.

Bright? Clear? Snow? But Niamh had cancer, really quickly. Didn't know it could be like. That. Didn't realise cancer could be. So sudden. But Niamh had it already, didn't she? And then that scan. Nia remembered Ike speaking in the shop. Yes, they were in the changing room for part of it, weren't they? Bit awkward. No space there. Someone had left a scarf… Lovely silk, not one of theirs. A grey pattern. Would look good on Siân. No, not ever silk in *Extraordinaria*… Not their thing.

Ah, still hot. Still hot… Scalding. *Skalds* were stories, weren't they? From Iceland? Never been there, either. But Ike had come in on Monday morning, when Skye had taken Ffrez over to playschool and Nia had been working out the change in the till. Hadn't she? Not enough pound coins, yes. She felt frustrated because of that… There was so much to do, running a shop… Washing the windows next. The summer light showed the dust, the wind's kisses.

Serene had worked the till that Saturday afternoon and she was capable. Oh yes. But she had forgotten to transfer the cash to the safe. No money kept overnight was one of the rules

Nia was introducing after months of bad practice. But fair play...Serene was...

Yet that scan had showed so many... *what?*

No, she was in the changing room with Ike standing outside. Hadn't really opened, had she? Some people always rushing. Ike was one... But she heard the bell on the door and Ike was already inside and talking to her... Her favourite postman had even given Ike the letters. And Ike was still holding them. Like cards in his fist. Didn't know where to put...

On the counter, here? he'd called.

What..?

So this is where you hide, is it? he'd asked.

This is where you go?

Hide?

When you slip away from Skye?

Ha.

You're allowed.

I know that.

Hey, that Serene chick is...

Hands off, boyo. Don't even think it.

Good legs. Could be a dancer...

Forget it. Think about money instead. There's a big room upstairs. You could pay us rent. Great view. Not the sea, though.

But Nia had been keen to get on... Ike had a hangover, didn't he? The night before he'd been to one of the new bars that had opened in the old coal warehouse. And yes, she'd come out and made coffee for him.

Here, have this. With a glass of water. Filled it twice... That Belgian beer, he said. *Butcher's tears,* she remembered that. The new bar down at the harbour. *Yr Harbwr,* they'd called it. Oh yes... But how Manners had laughed. Old school, see. Old school. Didn't like...

Belgian yet imported from Amsterdam. Or so Ike said. Small world, he'd said. Small world... Yes, that was it...

Then serves you right, she'd laughed...

But the scalding bath, that's what she recalled. As hot as Niamh could bear. Every day, hot as this one. With coconut oil in the water. And cannabis oil, as much as Ike could afford... So many places to smoke it, he'd said. But not all the coffee shops, not all the places sell the oil. Specialty purchase, that...

Trying anything, weren't they? said Ike. Faith healing, old wives' tales. Yes, lots of truth from those old wives. Ancient wisdom.

Extraordinaria was full of ancient wisdom.

But tumours, was it? Yes, Ike had said they were black on the screen. Black speckles. Everywhere. All over Niamh, all over her white body. *Speckling?* What was the word Ike used?

Ah, my poor thrush.

That was the phrase Ike had spoken. That Monday morning in the shop. Not properly ready, even, were they? But she heard the bell so the door must have been open. *Ah, my poor...*

Any age, he'd told her. Even Ffresni, he'd said. Young as Ffrez. And Nia had been startled. Sometimes Isaac Pretty could get too close, too close... Even to use Ffresni's name. In that context.

But every day. Twice a day, as hot as Niamh could bear. And the bathroom smelling so wonderfully he said. The coconut oil, the cannabis oil, the hot water. Through her skin, they hoped. And the air already saturated… The air…the sweet, the medicinal…

Like jewellery, Ike had said. Black jewels on Niamh's skin. What the scan showed. Her wonderful skin that smelled of coconut, that smelled of… *Ah my poor thrush.*

Yes, that cough was passing but Ffresni still with a rattle in her chest. A toy, wheezing. We go wrong, we go wrong and then and then…

But cancer? It seemed to follow Ike. Didn't it? Poor Niamh. With her black jewels. She must be dead? Why hadn't Ike said so. But if she's alive…where is she now? Amsterdam? No, she'd died. And that guitarist he mentioned? They'd all talked about music they liked. Dead too. Cancer? Kick out the… That's the real motherfucker. Because Dai Pretty also. What had been Dai's problem?

Siân had told her. All those dry cleaning chemicals… *Easy Street*? Oh God, yes. Easy Street. Siân's friend. Dad's friend. No wonder Ike Pretty's running round the world. He knows he's being chased…Yeah, maybe that explains it. Explains Isaac Pretty… But maybe he's carrying it with him…

The pain in Nia's side was a white stitch, suddenly in the chest, and now a white carbide flash through the skull.

She surfaced in the darkness.

Into the blackness of The Shwyl.

84

Prehistoric blackness

Not even a candle. Ever in that world.

The taste of lavender was now the taste of limestone...

Gasping.

XIV

Hey.

If she made a move she would step on a snake. The sand was covered with black adders and no space to squeeze between, no place to, no space...

She was paralyzed.

Ni?

She tried to turn over.

Nia!

There was Skye's face above her in the dawn light, a dawn that was dark. On a day that didn't exist...

Whaat? she mumbled.

Today!

Day?

The day...

What day...?

D Day. Departure... Get ready....

Nia's mind was full of snakes. Adders in the sand, the trails they left, the skins they sloughed. Adders, she'd dreamed. But not death adders. Oh no, not them. Only one girl on The Caib had ever died from a viper bite, the girl in the dunes, years ago.

It's almost like she's still sleeping, someone had said, when they discovered her, a child with her cheek in the sand. Upon its hot quilt. Not a mark, they said. Unblemished by the snake's tooth.

Or was that the child in the dunes, millennia ago?

No, that child's bones were burned, her body facing south under the slab. A body curled like a sea louse. In the stone cist. A body like a broken hoola-hoop. Yet someone had wept for her. Somebody must have wept…

The coffee cup was waiting where it always did, and from the curtain's crack a marine light was seeping into her mind. A ragged hem. Again, mother of pearl was creeping along the bed.

Skye shimmied down and licked the gold hair on the girl's belly.

No! Nia said. Oh God. You're right. Ffrez? She's still sleeping?

Of course. And just one minute for us.

No, insisted Nia. I hate myself. That's over. Find a cock to suck… Where's Carpenter when you need him?

Look, said Skye, I've been up hours…

And I've been having another dream. Horrible, as ever. Let's bundle the sheets up. We'll put a wash on, Serene can peg out. But snakes all over the sand. Coming out of the dune. Jesus, coming out of the springs…

That black adder you saw, said Skye. They've always been around… But it scared you…

No, it's the heat. Do snakes hibernate for thirty years? It's all different now. Something's happened…

Skye was pulling off the twin sheets. It seemed she'd slept in the armchair in her faded Saskatoon Blades tee shirt.

Then Ffrez's things. All those vests. She hasn't worn the

tights, too hot. But the lovely yellow dress on its own...
Leggings too.

Thought you soaked that dress, said Skye.

Bad mother, am I?

...What?

XV

They came out of the office into the sound of running water and walked down a passage painted green. There was a ruined plastic desk there, stuffed with papers, its surface scarred by cigarette burns.

The corridor curved to the right and it was soon unpainted and darker. The sound of water was louder here, the floor puddled and air cool. Everywhere there were holding tanks and piping, some of it bright copper, the rest ancient. Some might have been lead.

That's it, said Skye. The sound of the spring...

The resurgence, corrected the pumping station official. But it's low. Lower than I've ever known. And I've been here thirty years. Very near.

Feels as if I'm underground already, joked Skye.

You are.

The water sound was now like a bath being filled. The passage curved again to the right and they emerged in a high chamber cut out of the rock. Or perhaps it was a natural cavern.

Here we are, said the guide.

The passage was immediately blocked by a metal gate. Nia thought it might be twenty feet high. It was familiar but she couldn't say from where...

This is where it starts, added the guide.

Or finishes, said Skye.

Yeah, so far it's the main entrance, said Ike. But there have to be others blocked by sand and rock. As we know.

Wow, said Skye. This will do me.

The others were looking at their equipment stacked against the gate. But Nia was staring at the gate itself.

Where does the water come from? No, really? asked Skye.

Springs? Some of it. Rivers? Some of it. And rain of course. Some of it. Bit of a mystery as to all of it. No, there's no right answer for all of it.

The man looked at Ike's steelies.

Like your shoes, he said. Nice colour. Get ruined down here.

XVI

The tide was out, as far out as the girl could remember. This was farther out, people said, than it had ever been.

Why, she had once asked her father, does the sea disappear? And why does it come back?

The mouth of the pipe was exposed with its iron grille. This pipe was banded in iron and brick, restored in concrete. She had often looked into it but now stood peering into its mouth. A cave entrance, she considered. There were plenty of caves around The Caib, crevices and fissures in the lime. The dunes were a honeycomb of passageways under the sand...

But this was the deepest and most dangerous cave. Once she had called out and her voice vanished in a series of echoes.

Hey! Hey Hey.

You! You You.

Hey.

You.

HEY!

YOU!

A man had come up behind her and said, no, you can't go in there. Come away.

Why? she asked.

Because. That's why. It's the sewer pipe. You never know what's going to come out... You can't go into places like that...

And he had stalked off. She turned again to the grille, the black mouth, the encrustations.

You, she heard.

Low.

Hollow...

The deepest note on the piano.

Halloo...

Yoou...

She shook her head, thinking about the grille. It was famous, with letters of complaint about it in the press every summer. Usually it was hung with debris, a portcullis streamered with bunting.

Not long ago a child had vanished into the pipe. A little girl had climbed through the bars and vanished into that annulus. Someone had reported it and a search been made. But nothing was found. Nothing like a child, at least.

So the alarm must have been mistaken, although the woman who reported the incident remained adamant. A girl had pushed through the grille, she said. And climbed in.

She had been seen, against the sun, the filthy lozenges of the grille printed black against her school uniform. That blue check dress, the maroon blazer. A schoolgirl walking into the sewer pipe.

★

Skye was ahead. Nia could hear the chink of her equipment. A sound she supposed never heard in this place. But Ike must have been moving quickly. It was difficult to keep up. She paused and switched off her torch.

The taste of darkness, its press upon her. Under the blankets at home. But there was no home here. This place had been waiting for her. For them all... She switched the torch back on. Skye was rustling ahead.

Nia found they were singing.

Red eyes.
White faces.
Red mouths.

She wasn't sure how it had started but she liked it. Music down here. Music never heard before. The beat was her own blood.

When the passage became lower they sank to their knees. All wore neoprene protectors but it was difficult progress. Ike, leading, some way ahead, threw instructions over his shoulder. But when they found themselves crawling Nia's worst fears had come true. So soon.

For her, the passage was part of a crevice in the limestone that might widen or narrow impossibly. What did he call them? *Rifts*, was that the word?

More than once she felt her helmet scrape the cave roof. She found she was pulling herself along, sometimes the limestone pitted with grykes or ridged like railway sleepers.

At least it's dry, Ike called.

So far, grunted Skye.

Hey? said Skye, later.

The reply took a long time.

Shouldn't we be roped?

Their voices were thin and distant.

Why aren't we roped? called Nia.

There was no answer from Ike.

Anything to film? called Nia a little later, not expecting a reply.

Some kind of flue, she heard Skye to say, repeating Ike's words. The pair ahead were vanishing into darkness. She found there were pieces of wood to push past, one branch still showing growth. It was holm oak, its leaves like leather. Sandpapery, she thought. She knew it from the dunes.

Maybe after five hundred yards, with a pause half way, she realized the crevice was widening. It had not become a squeeze. There had been a stretch when she found herself covered in moonmilk but that now seemed over.

Nia looked at the sleeves of her boiler suit. Grey with dust, that strange limestone ash in her mouth and nostrils, at the back of her throat. She recalled something Ike had once said. About the Dead Sea scrolls. Which he claimed were found in caves. So many unexplored places, he'd said. But how might, she wondered, anyone imagine what had not yet been discovered...?

★

When they halted she felt exhausted. The others laughed aloud at themselves as Nia dragged herself in.

Grey as corpses, Ike said.

Aren't we? said Skye. Fucking clowns, anyway.

I'm enjoying it, lied Nia. Sorry I'm so far behind. Sick of looking at Skye's boots.

Over four hours, that took, said Skye.

You were both great, said Ike.

Red eyes, white faces, red mouths, Nia breathed to herself. Skye repeated the whisper and all three began to use it again.

Red eyes.
White faces.
Red mouths.

Closer to five, really, Nia said. But hearing their voices, even oddly compressed, made her feel better.

Ike returned eventually from a further reconnaissance.

Good news, he said.

Ten yards further on, the crevice leveled out.

It was as if for those four hours they had been ascending a low slope.

Use your lights, he said. Ahead shone a black surface.

Water, Skye said first. I've been wondering where it's all gone...

Cave pool, Ike said, almost triumphantly. As if he had guessed it might be there. The three stood on the side of a hollow maybe twenty feet wide. It gleamed like tar in their nightsearchers.

This is big, Ike said.

The pool lay in what seemed a natural crater. Its edges were black mud. There might have been two islands in that limestone lagoon, but Nia's torch picked out something embedded closer to her feet.

She took a step down, felt the surface was firm enough, and continued. When she returned she showed what she'd picked up.

Amazing, laughed Skye. How...?

Don't believe it, said Ike.

Touch it!

Okay, I do.

Nia held a red Costa takeaway coffee cup. She turned it round to show printed on the side was 'The UK's favourite coffee shop'.

How...? asked Skye. How the hell....

Easy, said Nia. Come down a stream and into the cave system.

Yeah, said Ike. It's not as if there was takeaway coffee in the stone age... When your cave artist friends were knocking about.

The cup was filled with black sludge.

Seems someone likes it strong, said Skye.

Last year, probably, said Nia. In all those rains.

Or maybe some caver in the system upstream. Cavers can be real arseholes... This bloke in uni...

They've tested the waters here, said Ike. Used to be suitable for drinking. Now pesticides and slurry rule that out. Usual things. Can't keep it pollution free. In wet weather that climb might be impossible.

We'd be underwater, said Skye.

Shine the torches, said Nia.

They stood on the lake's edge and illuminated the surface. There was driftwood at the edge, at Nia's feet what might have been a willow branch. As they looked more closely they picked out spars and boughs that seemed to have come from the sea.

Well, don't sound so surprised, said Ike. There's a maze of stream above our heads that feed into rivers. And those rivers flow into the sea.

And stuff comes up river with high tides, said Nia.

But underground, said Skye.

Deep under, said Nia. She stepped out again to the water's edge and bent her head to taste the lake water. Lapping from her cupped hand.

Well, it's not salty.

Fresh, said Ike. Remember, six million gallons of fresh water per day. It's used as back up for us.

Let's walk to the other side, said Nia. I once went to the museum to see that lake hoard they discovered. Bronze cauldrons, bits for horses...

Yes?

Oh yes. Grave goods left for the departed. Or for the gods.

Sweet, said Ike.

And swords. Frail as leaf skeletons... All those precious things...

Or maybe our god just fancies a Costa, said Ike. Yeah, yeah, I know....

Not just the gods of the lake, said Nia. It was about...

What? asked Ike.

Belief, said Skye.

Yes, said Nia. Didn't have to be faith.

With that Ike knelt down on the lakeside and pretended obeisance.

Listen, laughed Nia. I'm thinking of those two thousand buried springs. Two thousand years of pollen. All presented to Maponos, not the great god Costa.

Looks eerie, the black lake, said Ike. I'll give you that. *Espresso*-coloured. Might imagine an arm rising up, waving a sword.

Could be bottomless, said Skye.

Hardly, said Ike. But might be all kinds of rubbish at the bottom. Probably at its lowest level for years, just now. Decades. Good time to explore...

Nia licked her palm again. Well, we wouldn't die of thirst in here, she said. Pesticides or not...

Still on his knees, Ike intoned

red eyes
white faces
red mouths

There's bound to be waterfalls here at wet periods, he said. Swallets, as they say.

As Johnny Tarr might say, that is, said Skye.

Forget him.

Sorry.

The women smiled at one another in the dark.

That passageway reminds me of arroyos in the desert, said Skye. Boy, they can flood quickly. Deadly.

This bit of The Shwyl might be like a bath with the plug permanently out, said Ike.

Or a bath with several plugs, said Nia. Hey, it's a beach underground.

River beach, said Ike.

Even sand on it, said Skye.

And why not? There's thousands of ways for water to get in and out.

Nia was looking at her own footprints in the mud.

Why not indeed? asked Ike. So, camp, girls.

Watch it!

Think you've earned it. Least your knees have.

★

The lake lay behind a wall of calcite. This looked like dirty ice in the LED. They stretched out and shared a thermos but Ike was soon up, discovering what lay in the shadows.

Pools, he said, out of the darkness. Rock pools, I suppose.

What else is there? the women asked when Ike emerged. He'd walked into the lagoon.

Huh, he said. Sand.

That all?

Sort of quicksand. Was up to my knees.

Oh, said Nia. Sorry.

Think it's really a stream bed. Some bones there too. Maybe horse, they're big enough.

Horse? Down here? asked Nia. Are you crazy?

Maybe used for food, said Skye.

Well, there's a skull. Might be a horse. Kind of wedged between rocks. Yeah, might be a horse.

How?

Somebody carried the meat down.

Oh.

Horses didn't live down here?

Probably not.

But there were pit ponies hundreds of feet down mines, said Nia.

Food, I'd say, said Ike.

Most like.

Yeah?

Sure to be.

But…a horse?

Horse's skull, said Ike.

Nia came over and shone her light into the water.

Watch out for cave shrimps, said the man. If they're here they'll be white. Transparent almost, poor wee beasties.

What else might be around, called Skye.

Maybe nothing.

Don't say that.

More likely there'll be nothing.

Nothing?

Nothing is the usual condition.

Oh...

Space is full of nothing.

Don't say that.

The world is full of nothing.

Shut up.

As to dark matter, we can't see it. Yet. But dark matter might be nothing too. Turn your light off and check how dark it is.

Oh yes.

Life in a black hole.

Blind fish maybe? asked Skye.

Or nothing. Well, in the threshold zone perhaps. Look, we came what seemed the obvious route. But there must be other ways to get here. There usually are.

What about crabs? asked Nia.

This is freshwater, said Ike.

So?

So try the Philippines. Not here.

But up above you find lots of little white crabs, said Nia. Little ghosties, you know. The rock pools are full of them...

Ones I see are always dead, said Skye.

OK, look out for bones, said Ike. In the driftwood.

Of...?

Cave lion, maybe?

Oh yes...

Well...horse. Now.

Bear too.

Don't tell me...

Human?

No!

Maybe this was home for all sorts in the past, said Ike. Could have been a hyena den... Depends how far back you want to go. Or...

Or dinosaurs? laughed Skye.

Or like I said, nothing. Simple as that. Nothing is everywhere. Unless you're after real rudimentary things. And neither of you is an ecologist...

Ooh, said Skye, flashing her torch over the rock pool, I think I just saw a horse. Or was it a hyena. Or...?

Yeah, said Ike. I heard it laughing...

Skye took off her helmet and rubbed her hair.

She and Nia had packed peanut butter mixed with honey to spread on crackers. They'd also prepared their own energy bars with raisins and cooking chocolate. Ike was eating from a packet of salami, which he offered round. Then he split a pack of Mars bars.

No thanks, said Nia. Yet. We got Kumari banana chips to come...Skye discovered them in Kerala. Fantastic. Oh, and dried apricots, dried pineapple, sesame balls...

Which I discovered in the Co-op, said Skye.

Suit yourselves.

How many meals down here? she asked.

Say six. Seven? Eight if we're hungry.

Not many, is it?

We won't starve....

Sure of that?

Yeah, famous last words...

What's for tea?

Ha, said Nia. Dried chick peas and rice. Again the Kerala touch. Wish I'd been there.

You will.

What did the hyenas eat?

Ike smirked under the torchlight. Anything.

Such as?

Worms. Woodlice. Grasshoppers. Grass.

Dead hyenas?

In here?

Ike shrugged.

Grasshoppers in here?

Ike shrugged again. Slugs too, he smiled, red-eyed.

And anything dead? said Nia.

Before they died out.

Rabbits?

But there weren't any rabbits then, were there? asked Nia.

Rabbits are recent, said Ike.

Why did the hyenas die out?

No rabbits.

No, why?

Climate, said Ike. We had ice ages, you know...

But grass?

You'd eat grass if you were hungry enough.

People still do.

People will.

That mad poet, said Skye. He ate grass.

They all ate grass, said Ike. Those mad poets. Weed, wasn't it? What was the other one? Laudanum? Magic mush? All those insane sonnets…

We've all done it, said Nia. As to real grass, cats eat grass to make themselves sick. And dogs do. And Nebudchadnezzar, he ate grass for seven years. Or something like that.

The starving eat grass.

Refugees.

That death march. You know…

So many fucking death marches…

Auschwitz? murmured Nia. Your pictures?

Don't know, said Skye.

And when the grass is gone? said Ike. What then? Mars anybody? Oh go on.

No ta.

Eat your principles, then.

★

Oh, said Nia. Guess what.

Yes?

It's voting?

Is it?

Today?

Thursday. And Thursday's over.

Oh well.

Voting?

Forget about it...

Oops..

Is Thursday over...?

Up there, yes, said Skye.

Well gone.

Unreal...

...Yeah... Unreal...

Meant to.

Me too.

But down here it never was Thursday...

★

Slowly all three sat down at the side of the pool.

Still don't know how, said Skye, but there's plenty of drift-wood around.

Fancy a fire? asked Ike.

No.

No? You're right. But thousand year old driftwood is possible. Gradual accumulation. Or older, much older. They've found driftwood in caves with hyena and bear bones. Though cave air is usually humid, so wood decays quick.

So, relic driftwood? asked Skye.

Yeah. Like relic populations of creatures long thought

extinct.

Oh wow, said Skye sitting back. Not here though?

Not in The Shwyl, laughed Nia.

What lies beneath, eh? said Ike almost to himself, unwrapping another mini-mars.

Fire and ice, he said eventually. That's what it was all about. Any people who wanted these caves would have to get rid of the hyenas or the cave lions or...

The other people, said Nia.

Yeah. Suppose so.

Yeah, probably other people.

How many people were there? asked Skye.

Not many. Considering how many there are these days. People were rare. And always endangered.

Did people live down here? asked Skye.

Ike shrugged. Maybe. It's possible. You think we're a long way in but these passages could go on for twenty miles. Fifty. Kind of a labyrinth. We're just skimming it...

Think there's a minotaur? breathed Sky.

Nope. But there've always been mazes. One day there'll be maps of this place. Like the London tube.

One day we might need to live down here, said Nia.

Good chance, said Skye.

When you stop moving you realize it's cold, Nia added. Not shivery, but not like it must have been up top today. Eighty, Serene guessed from the forecast. Said you're going to miss the best of it. She still doesn't understand...

Nia stood up and flashed her torch over the pool water and

back to the lake. She could hear her boots scraping on sand. But what she was listening to was seepage, the actual creation of dripstone.

Once, there was the splash of stone falling into one of the pools. The two other explorers looked up from their meal.

Nia ran her fingers down the nearest wall. It wouldn't have surprised her to find chitons there, those crawling things she'd known all her life. Like rock themselves, those creatures. Sea lice. All they wanted was to stay where they were. A little like her.

She thought there was black mould on this rock. Near the entrance they'd used there had been plenty of moss but as The Shwyl grew darker this had disappeared.

So, here I am, she said. And she continued to listen. Water was pittering like a rainstick. All around her it was percolating out of the limestone. Even in a drought, she thought. Even...

Would we be protected from radioactivity? she asked.

Well more so than up top... After all we're buried. Pretty deep. Must be half a mile of limestone hanging over your head. Good job you're not claustrophobic.

XVII

She switched off the beam.

Then back on.

They carried nightsearchers and headtorches, though there was a Pulser and a Fenix for main lighting. The women wore battery belts, and all three backpacks.

Nia held an Edison, *nightsearcher* being a word she had come to love. It comforted, as she shone it round *Extraordinaria* after hours, as if in search of intruders.

How often she'd read the manufacturer's description of the torch: *Ultra bright long life LEDS with optical lens to produce a clear white light. Positive push button operation. All joints sealed with 'O' rings.'*

Yes. They were trusting Ike, but the equipment was more important. She read again the description of her Unilite flash-light: *PS-FL3 200 Lumen white Luxeon LED, 136m beam range, flood to spot focus control, 3 stage dimming function plus defence strobe.*

Hey, Princess Leia! Skye had said earlier. What you need is a light sabre! Yet Nia liked the word 'lumen'. Because that's what they were, three luminaries, leading the way.

But going where?

Lux meant light, didn't it? As well as soap? And candela was candlepower? Good old candles, carry your own firelight. Maybe they should take burning brands down. Wreckers in the town had tied brands to cattle horns. That was the legend, but Nia imagined the cows would have gone crazy...

Legends were like that, another dodgy technology. But fire meant light and light was the key. And *defence strobe* sounded good. The poetry of light, Skye noted. But then Nia stopped reading as there was too much to deal with.

She switched off the torch.

★

Nia had always loved wells. The town was famous for its wells. Old maps indicated *walls* and *wells,* and once, *remains of a tower.*

But there was...nothing, really. Even history lay buried. *Area of drifting sand* was what the maps said. With a symbol of black dots... Her dunes, as Ike suggested, were filled with nothing... Even language was sparse.

If people explored properly, Skye had said, they might discover underground links to The Shwyl. The week before they'd taken Ffrez to the nearest well and told her to make a wish. Skye had given the child a penny, dated 1897, big and black and smooth as glass, the face of Victoria still clear.

Nia protested that it might be valuable but Skye insisted and the child had dropped the coin into the darkness. Nia made her own wish. All pretended they heard a splash but understood the drought was affecting the well water.

Whatever you wish for, said Skye. But there's not a penny-
worth down there.

★

Nia switched the torch back on.

Every one of her pockets was stuffed with batteries. She
had begun to check her zips, caressing herself for reassurance
that the batteries were still there. But that didn't mean the
batteries would work. Did it? Each battery she carried had
been tested the previous day.

Yet dread accompanied her from the first step after the gate,
the gate across the streambed that was the entrance. There was
not a drop in that stream now. Even the mud was dry. This
happened, Nia knew. Sink holes in the limestone might appear
and swallow whole rivers. Gone as if by evaporation.

She switched off the torch.

What she saw was stained glass, each fragment distinct yet
black. It was so dark that Nia felt she could see better with
eyes closed. The more tightly she shut her eyes the happier
she felt.

The Milky Way of her mind. Red giants like Beetlejuice
swimming before her... Galaxies that were spiderwebs. But
were there spiders here in The Shwyl...? There must be...
There were spider webs over the desk in the entrance and

there were webs over the gate, but she's seen no others yet.

And the torch back on.

But were there bats in the cave? There were motes in the beam. Spots before her eyes. Dots on the maps? *Areas of drifting sands.* Unclassified. Unrecorded. No words. No language ever in this place. She switched off the torch.

Then on.

Then off.

The darkness was electric.

She thought about what they were saying. The first words uttered. Ever, down here. Dripping of limewater, rise and fall of levels in the limewater sumps, sounds never heard because no ear was present to hear. Thunderstones for the stone deaf. No, all sounds were suffocated now.

★

Then on.

★

Then off.

★

Only touch.

Now touch was all.

Cold the cave, its darkness something she could taste.
An oil of darkness.
She could roll it round in her mouth like a marble.
Her nipple in her child's mouth...

And Ffresni always closed her eyes when she sucked...

★

Or something oozing from the rock, this darkness, from the
fissures. Underwater, she felt herself. But that sound? The sea-
sound in the stone.Every breath from every lily, the lilies that
left limestone.

There had been trillions but beyond everything she could
taste was darkness. That bloodstone dark. This bloody dark.
Drenched in blood, this dark.

When she touched the torch she held it like a lover's hand.
No, like Ffresni's hand. And there in the darkness were the
batteries beside it. *All the paraphernalia of light.* Cool, like the
stone. Cold the water. But she was falling, she was falling
through limestone halls, the vaulted rooms, through the
crypts, black scum on the walls, the lichen in her hair, dreaming of...

Quickly she realized they would have to get out. Before darkness suffocated them all. But if she screamed who would hear?

The two others were ahead. Almost naturally she had adopted third place. Looking at Skye's backside. Her boot soles with the capital D.

Like a railway here, said the older woman. So uneven…

She could hear snatches of Ike's talk:

I expect…the temperature to be comfortable. Say about 10 Centigrade… It'll stay like that. Not that we… Don't expect we'll go… really deep. I think roughly north-west… Not that we…

Nia noted he wasn't wearing his headtorch. Again disobeying his own orders, Isaac Pretty. Mr Cool.

Christ…

★

But maybe it wasn't so bad. They made slow progress. As ever Nia found it easier to be elsewhere. In her mind the sand was blowing west to east. The field of the beach was grey, the sand making eskers wherever it drifted. And the light blinding, so the sand was yellow becoming white. Like ancient straw, she thought, never turned.

The heat had brought jellyfish on to the beach. There were thousands of blue discs and larger moon jellyfish. Nia felt compelled to stare into their flesh. She knew them of old, had been brought up with moonies.

Those purple veins within? she wondered. Jelly hearts? Jelly brains? Some of the moon jellyfish could be enormous. With thalidomide arms and legs.

She thought of The Fish... Still working in the Kingdom after all these years. Selling tickets to people who wanted to be frightened. Marooned on the beach, those jellyfish. Strange placentas...

Or, Nia thought, her mother's hair. Siân's hair was grey, a bush of bonfire smoke. How quickly that had happened.

She'd arrange a cut soon. Siân would never accept colouring, but a cut would sculpt her face. And next visit, she'd take Siân to the bathroom and wash her hair. Give her a deep bath. Make her smell of rosepetals and lavender and not the usual ward.

She remembered Siân scrumbling lavender bath cubes at her own bathtime. Did people use cubes anymore? Siân had talked of fields of lavender in Provence.

We'll go, she had laughed. One day... *Easyjet* to Toulon. Or is it Toulouse?

Her mother had grown lavender in her allotment. Blue as dusk, Siân's lavender. Or the cobalt of a June midnight. She always said the last thing she saw when leaving that garden late was lavender. Its smoke smearing the air. Bats darting, the cricket drone and the lingering of lavender on her fingers and thumb. Lavender the colour of lovehearts.

Or they could sell bath cubes in the shop. There were already incense sticks and she and Skye had burned one last night. No, two nights ago. No, no! Three.

114

What day was it now? But her incense stick had flared like a firework, leaving that morning a perfect pyramid of ash... Yesterday morning? No, two days ago... Maybe three...

Nia remembered her mother's skin in the lavender light, its oil on Siân's thighs. Maybe a root or two in newspaper left as gifts. That had been Nia's job in their old street.

★

I've been a trespasser all my life, Nia had said once. Feeling I didn't belong. Maybe that I didn't belong anywhere. It was as if I was stealing something not mine. Time, maybe. Yes, time. And, yes, that's thrilling. Maybe it's shocking. Maybe it's how everybody feels about life.

Because the dunes was the place for trespassing. In my head the dunes can't belong to anyone, even when they built houses on those twelve acres.

Why did they do that?

To protect the rest. Even when all the plastic is washed up by the tide. Or when beer cans are crushed into the sand of the source. The dunes are still wild even when the people I meet there are only trying to get a mobile signal.

You know, she said, I once met a man wearing headphones. Over there. Over here. I wanted to say, I wanted to tell him, if you listened, sir you'd hear what a whitethroat sounds like. But he was gone.

A whitethroat? Skye had repeated.

Yeah. They haven't come back either.

★

As a child she had hidden under the bedclothes, loving the darkness. Or made a den with dolls. Sometimes there were tea parties beneath the blankets, and Nia would smile and sing to herself, ignoring the Vines who called and treated her as lost.

When John and Siân Vine came into her room they pretended not to know she was there: beneath the sheets, humming her songs.

Now I lay me down to sleep.

Or

Pretty maids all in a row.

Once Siân had pulled back the blankets and said, found you! It had been startling. That was not supposed to happen. Nia believed she had cried. No, she'd be sure never to do that with Ffrez.

Sometimes nine and sometimes ten.

What was that about? She'd look it up in her nursery rhyme books.

But it hadn't been really dark. Not that Nia was afraid of the darkness. In the college caving team, she'd never been daunted by squeezes or chokes.

What she had loved was cave breath, the evidence of hidden passageways. Yes, the breath that could flow from limestone. Its kiss on her cheek. The cool current that pulled her forward.

Like a fan engine, she remembered John Vine saying. When they pumped air into mineshafts. For those forced to work underground. Or dig the tunnels.

Darkness was nothing, even when her dolls were buried at the far end of the bed.

Under the haystack, fast asleep.

No, there was a comfort there even when it was harder to breathe. All Nia had to do was hold her breath and turn her face to the flow, to the air that might have travelled miles underground. To that kiss. Sweet as Ffresni's breathing. For Nia, the consecration of caving. The subterranean wind that lifted the cave smell.

She had noted that smell at once. Earth and wet stone. A limestone perfume. Yet humid, that honeycomb. Didn't history smell like that? Its dripping library.

Didn't the grave...?

She understood time was different in caves. The first occasion she had gone underground, she had sensed new time. Geological time. Yes, the equipment was strange enough, the ropes and clinking karabiners, the LED torches, the waterproofs and wetsuits, the orange neoprene.

Yet despite the group she had joined being talkative to a fault, Nia had begun to understand cave time. Companions had pointed out fossils in a sheet of flowstone, the calcite glittering in torchlight. She had realised she was one of the first people to see those creatures, whatever they were. Locked as if within glass. A child's sketches. Ffresni's little masterpieces on the fridge door. Meaningless scribbles.

So too the shapes in the dripstone. The torches' white arcs had revealed a series of dungeons and rimstone pools. Not unlike, she thought, The Horns and its boulders. Or the lip of The Chasm where she and her friends had dived.

Yet always beyond those beams was the realm of darkness. So thick it suffocated light. Torchbeam or carbide glow, light was puny compared to what it penetrated. Shrapnel from a brief explosion? Light might cling to the cavern but it was fleeting. Some caves were large enough for concerts by symphony orchestras. But The Shwyl could not be like that. The Shwyl was smaller. And somehow more...*pagan,* she thought. Which was comforting.

★

Rain on lilies, that's what Nia saw. Maybe limestone was made of black lilies. The brush of lilies upon her breasts and throat. That was caving. Oh, and belts and harnesses and white LED. It was up to her to dream what lay in The Shwyl. It was unexplored and unknown. Somehow squirming through, they'd find...

Skye was adamant. We'll go no further than we need, she had insisted. As if there could be a choice. Sure to be blocked solid, thought Nia. Boulders that required chiseling or levering. Sometimes there was blasting. But count that out...

Even the thought of tiny amounts of explosive frightened Nia. Of course, it will be all dark zone, she considered. So the lighting generator and the torches had to be more than reliable. And they were, so far...

No-one has been where they were going. Their first twilight was hornblende. Then pitch. The first passageway was easy enough yet solid with sand and silence.

Rain on black lilies, that was The Shwyl. Black petals upon her eyes.
Never lifting...

XVIII

South of the sewer lay the sands. Beyond these were gutters of lime-stone never glimpsed. There were men out there now, armed with pikes to prise soft bodied crabs from the rock pools. These were considered best bait for sea bass. Anglers came to The Caib for shark or smooth-hound, and she had known ray fishermen, the usual hopefuls pursuing mullet. In the past there had been mackerel fishing from boats and there were now more locals trying their luck...

She opened her eyes. The world grew darker. She closed them again.

Black petals lay still upon her face, over her eyes. She opened those eyes a second time and the darkness became deeper...

She began to distinguish a shape. In front of the blackness was a series of metal bars, drilled into the rock of floor and ceiling.

Gradually she decided it was a gate. But it would not admit her. The bars were cold and black with rust. Behind them was the shape of an entrance in the rock. It was a cave.

Yes, cold and slippery. She could hear the sound of running water. As in every cave she knew this water hissed while it settled. Rock pool silence was not silence at all and this silence sang within her. She could hear her own heart and listened as if it was something that did not belong to her body. She felt she was outside herself.

The gate was solid. She knew she could not move the bars or squeeze between. She didn't even know why she wanted to pass through. Whether she was coming out or going in...

When she awoke again it was still dark...

★

Nia knew if she took off her sandals the dune would be too hot. Kneeling down she sifted a handful of grains.

She could hardly bear it and guessed she was being burned. Here on the crest the view was immense as she squinted into the sun in the south, eyes full of lightnings.

There was sand in her hair and around her mouth, sand between her toes. Yes, sometimes she kissed the sand. Silk it seemed. Wasn't sand her lover, after all?

This was Nia's element. It was her world. She was made of its grit, its gilt, the grains of the coming twilight. She was born into sand and her life was a dream of sand, wind and sand. Yes, harsh this place that never relinquished its dreamers.

No, it never let go. Even Skye had returned, Skye who might have settled herself anywhere, Skye and her blue lenses that waited on the shelves in her studio she was creating above *Extraordinaria*.

★

Sparks floated around her. Jupiter in the south breathed like that starfish. She decided the group would go some time next week, up on the new ride. No arguments. As a kind of celebration they would view the town as they had never seen it before.

Above, the sunburned crowds surely continued, before turning away towards the arcades and the ranks of machines. To the gambling at Pozzo's, the booze in The Cat, the zombies looming out of a hundred screens. Or the new marina with its jetty crammed with tapas tables.

No, they protested. These people wanted to rise on the new ride. Its thrilling orbits. It had arrived with the new weather. Somehow from the first time it was erected it had been known as 'The Sunflower'. Orange and red, its metal spike towered over the fair. Then, it enlarged itself mechanically, with a flowering of ten different cars.

Never again, many said. Such heat was a benediction. This would always be a famous summer. The dust of history lay on the counter at The Cat and brimmed in the slots. Others shook their heads and muttered of warnings.

But most came because they wanted what they had considered impossible. A glimpse of themselves in a season that was making everybody famous. Each crowd was a thicket of selfie sticks.

Yes, they had to book a ride on The Sunflower. And for that they must speak to Virjilijs.

★

The light flickered over Skye's face. White, but then it went out. And came back. Ike nudged the generator and they were startled by Skye's appearance. White face, black body, eyes red glass...

That sand? she said. Was it white? White sand? Not like here anyway...

Hey, The Caib has white sand, laughed Nia. Just depends on the light. This summer it's white... Sometimes.

She might have dozed. When she awoke Skye was talking.

We'd walk down the beach, said Skye. Then back. Carp and I were kind of overcome with what we'd let ourselves in for. The markets, the *put-puts*. And God, those shitehawks...

All we get is the tides at *Extraordinaria,* said Nia, shaking herself. The sea like something electric, left on... Ffrez's lullaby...

First time I saw the crabs... added Skye, because you were talking about crabs, weren't you?

Think so.

Well, it was late afternoon. I remember we'd gone further than we ever did again. And the beach was red, the sand almost purple. And just before dark a crab appeared out of the sand. A ghost crab. And then, boy, there were hundreds of ghost crabs, hundreds and...

Oh please, breathed Nia.

I know, I know. That's how I felt. These things scuttling around. In and out of the sand. Sorry. We tried catching them but they were too clever. Vanished back into the beach, those ghosts disappearing, their eyes on stalks, waving their knives and forks.

Any crabs down here? asked Nia. I did ask! But we might be under the sea.

Unlikely, said Ike.

But how do you know?

Anyway, said Skye, I told Carp they gave me the creeps. But he laughed it off. Said it had been my idea to come. To India, to the Arabian Sea. I was looking at the fishing boats when the first crab just…appeared. From nowhere, pushing itself out of the sand…

Crabs in paradise, said Nia in shadow.

Then early evening, the second great installment of the day. People relieving themselves. Went to it in the mornings, then towards dark. Shitting on the beach.

Sounds reasonable, muttered Ike.

Oh yeah, said Skye. The sea's furious housekeeping will sort it out… Ever thought of life without a toilet?

Bit like down here, said Ike. Which reminds me. You've all got your toilet paper. I ticked that box. Thinking of you…

In the dark the women nodded.

Where no-one has shat before, added Ike. Bringing our humanity to a new world…

You sure nobody's ever been down? asked Skye. People

looking for coal? Iron? Mines can go back thousands of years.

Well, I can't be absolutely sure. But no evidence, if that's what you mean.

None?

No-one? So no coprolites.

You what?

Ossified turds, said Skye. Tell you a lot about history, do turds.

No absolute evidence until Tarr's only expedition. Johnny Tarr, pathfinder. Not that he went far. Probably not long enough for him to shit.

But we can't be sure, said Skye.

In his blog he wrote he was going to come back, but he'd been caught up in bigger projects.

Such as?

Well, that TV thing, the Indonesian caves...the New Mexico bat cave? Lucky bugger...

And here's you without a TV deal, laughed Skye. Don't worry, I'll make you look good.

But talking of necessities, said Nia, I remember Siân telling me about Hafn Bitw, when it was still lived in...

The petting zoo? asked Skye. The old buildings are ramshackle. Can't imagine...

Yeah, medieval squalor. I mean it. That farm just expired. The last people there were two old men, don't know how old. Siân thought eightyish at least. She used to trespass with her gang of friends. They were eight or nine and free to roam... Even I didn't get that. Dad was too neurotic...

John Vine was right, said Ike. The Caib's still full of fairground types. And don't look at me like that. I can see you. You know what I mean.

But what Siân remembers, continued Nia, is a kitchen table. A big board with these blue plates. She thinks it was like the blue china she dug up in her allotment. It was never ending, she said. Blue and white... And cats too. These cats on the table, eating cheese. The farmers inundated with cats and feeding them cheese and giving the last sheepdog saucers of tea... Yeah, this wall-eyed sheepdog lapping tea. Fly she was called.

Sounds right, said Ike.

And once, Nia said, she opened the door to the privy. It was a wooden hut outside the front door, which was always the back door. If you know what I mean...

Traditional in these parts, said Ike.

And a housemartin's nest under the roof. Said she felt she could almost reach up to it...

Why can't I remember this farm? asked Skye. The farm before the zoo.

You were East End, smiled Nia. Only the West End kids explored round there. Anyway, Siân said there was one of those old boys with a handful of straw. She said there were two holes in a wooden seat. Maybe they sat there together. Those two old men united in need. No water, of course. Wasn't on the mains so maybe they used the sea...

How? asked Ike. Okay, sometimes men pissed on a bale. But surprised they didn't go down to the rock pools. Like Skye says, at least the sea flushes stuff away...

But we're going to leave our visiting cards, laughed Nia. Our modest little coprolites. Yes, Siân loved that farm. Those cats and the tea-drinking sheepdog. Her own parents bought a dog off that farm and he drank tea as well. It was in his genes.

Sweet, said Skye.

But a ruin you say? That's why she loved it. Siân and John Vine together. There was a bog in the farmyard, might have been quicksand. My father said sometimes, if you listened, it sighed. And if you looked, sometimes it breathed. Like I did when I pretended to be dead...

You what? asked Ike.

Haven't you ever pretended that?

To be dead?

No.

It's great.

Pretended to be dead?

Yes.

Why? No, why?

Children do it all the time. Oh, forget it.

Nia settled herself against the rock, feeling chastised.

John Vine said...

Yeah?

He said he never dared walk out on it. Over its crater, over the weeds on the surface, over the horseshoe that never sank. The nails still in it! No, no matter how long the rain. He said he wondered what he might find if he could look under the surface, to see what it had swallowed.

Tyres, said Ike. Beercans.

No, in its hundreds of years. In its thousand. Someone like that man in the glacier.

What man?

He was on the news. His face black, pickled by cold.

Who...?

Johnnie Walker Black Label man.

Who the hell?

That black frost of whisky on his tongue.

Yeah! Who the hell...?

In the mountains.

A frozen man?

Yes!

Oh, Otzi? murmured Ike.

Who?

Otzi. Little dude in the Alps. Tattooed warrior.

Oh yes, said Skye. That's him. Scanned him, didn't they. Found out so much.

John Vine said he could see him there, said Nia. That man. Beneath the surface. Waiting for him. In the bogwater. On the farm.

Like the girl, Nia said, he could picture in the whirlpool near The Chasm. Dad's father had told him the legend. Of the girl who had stepped into the whirlpool and been sucked down. Who had spun round slowly. Until only her hands were there. Her fingers. Waving from the whirlpool. I believed that story. On the days I believed my father...

Yeah, horseshoe nails, said Ike, red-eyed out of the shadows.

That's all you'd find. Drained it now, haven't they? Since it reopened.

No, still there, said Nia. Fenced off. In this dry weather there's nothing to see...

Dai Pretty told me about the farm, said Ike. Said those farmers had always been together. I mean long time together. So, they might have sat there...under the housemartins' nest... Two martin's eggs. Which are off-white by the way. Faint scribble on the shell. As I recall.

From your egg stealing days?

Not proud of it. But telling the truth. Usually three to a clutch.

So, those two old boys, smiled Skye in the dark. I like it.

That was the story, according to my dad, said Ike. Come on, it must have happened...

Siân used to tell me of the smells in that farm, said Nia. Tractor oil, she loved that. Used to sit with her back to the tractor wheel and breathe it in. And the little bits of hay they cut. Still doing that, right up till the very end.

Yeah?

Red clover in the hay, and all. Talking of nests, Siân found a wren's nest in their barn. Always said how perfect it was. How painstakingly made... A periwinkle flower, a Quality Street wrapper. The green triangle. That was Siân's word. *Painstakingly*.

Course it happened, said Skye.

What? asked Nia. Shitting together? How...er, sweet.

No, they were a couple, said Ike. It was well known.

129

Always happened, said Skye. What's wrong with that?

Nothing, ladies, nothing. Keep your cool. Just saying. Course it happened. Always did. If you think…

Just as long… said Skye out of the darkness.

What?

Well… just as long… the most important thing is…

What?

I mean a really important thing.

What? For Christ's sake.

As long as there was plenty of straw…

★

The three shifted positions, shuffling their shadows.

How are your feet? asked Ike.

Fine, said Nia.

Mine too, said Skye. Got the Dakotas on, she added.

Those steelies you bought in Sask? asked Nia.

Paid for a new pair last year, she replied. Love my Dakotas. All that snow over there. Months of it. I never thought… Why didn't I?

Bad planning, said Ike.

Carp had Dakotas too. Remember we went up to La Ronge. Long trip to this rez. He drove, but I was always too scared of driving over there…

Why? laughed Ike. Road up to La Ronge would have been empty…

I hear you. But that's me. Woodland Cree, I think, anyway.

On the rez. So, we walked out on to the lake…

That's a lot of water, said Ike. Lac La Ronge's bloody immense.

Tell me about it. Walked way out on the ice, both of us. Then came to a dodgy area and turned back. Ice was a different colour. We looked round and kind of…lost our nerve. Didn't know how deep the lake was. But, there were kids fishing…think for pickerel…

I've done that, said Nia. No, not fishing. Never dared. Never wanted. But one winter the slacks were solid… I just crept carefully across. And all the time I could imagine faces looking up at me out of the ice. Like in a school photo…

Yeah, said Ike. Those school photos…

Keeley and Kaleigh and…faces of the drowned. Strange…

She held the torch closer. All of them were wearing gloves, and Ike had provided wollen hats. Skye called them tukes, she didn't know why. It was a Canadian word. Above the seep and streambed there was some kind of mould on the limestone, but further away from the channel the rock was dry. In her torchlight there were horizontal marks that might have been scratches…

★

Hollow, Nia's words. Empty sketches of words. Surely the first time such sounds had ever been heard in this place.

But had any sounds at all been heard. Or made?

Hyena growl?

Cave lion roar?

The whispering of frightened children?

But in what language?

The whispering was in her head.

Nia was listening to the echoes. Neither Skye nor Ike seemed struck by how their voices sounded underground. Yet she marveled. Her voice crushed under stone, that voice another fossil.

And that pub, she remembered. On the edge of the dunes. There were sounds preserved in its walls. Recordists came from all over the world to listen to the old words, the human sounds. Through the *germanium* in the stone. Yes, a sound archive.

Birdsong.

A child crying.

A mother weeping as her son went to the gibbet that had stood outside the pub.

A sound going on forever...

★

Ike called another halt.

This looks deep, he said. Torch doesn't show the bottom.

Nia joined the others at a crater's edge. Their torch beams played over a black wall.

Like a shaft, said Skye. Just falling away. Not manmade, is it?

Old mine?

She picked up a pebble at her feet and dropped it in. The three waited for a splash. But heard nothing.

Ike tried another stone. Again they heard nothing.

Well, doesn't prove it's bottomless, he said. But, it seems... *sheer.*

Nia crouched at the shaft rim and felt a current of air on her face.

Cave breath, she said. She realized she was perspiring. But that breath on her face. The man on the path, the green man, his bleeding teeth, his... *I'm like you...I'm like you I am...* Why had he said that? That man of leaves. Why had he...? Why...?

I'll try, said Skye, and picked up a piece of limestone. This time Nia thought she heard water. And an echo of water. But she wasn't sure.

You know, Nia said, you know what you said?

Mmm? asked Ike.

That there were people down here years ago?

Maybe.

What would they have looked like?

Small, said Ike.

Very small, said Skye.

And...?

They wouldn't have lived in here all the time, said Ike. But might have been born here. If it was a refuge.

Yeah, said Skye. Hiding place.

So maybe they died down here?

Could have...

But people like us...?

Small. And like us.

Not pale then? the girl said.

Pale?

Like these roots are white without light. And cave fish can be white.

And blind, said Ike.

Salamanders too, said Skye.

So, little pale people?

Probably, said Ike. But not blind.

Not all the locals were white remember, said Skye. She was chewing on an energy bar.

How? asked Nia.

Hey, know your history, laughed the man. How many black people were washed ashore in the old days?

You mean...

Yeah, slaves. Real blackfolk. And there were the pirates...

Yeah?

Arab pirates. Barbary pirates.

Berbers, said Skye. Out of Morocco. Could have taken some of our ancestors as slaves to the Arab markets. And we could be mixed up with those black slaves who came this way...

Oh.

Think of the prairie, said Skye. Those Ukrainian children burnt together. At least they had names. The slaves died unknown. And don't ask about Kerala...

Well then, think of all the ships wrecked here, said Nia. Don't tell me there was no sex trafficking...

No-one's denying it, said Ike. The past's a wild country...

No wilder than now.

Yeah, slaves, said Skye. New York's full of modern slaves.

London, said Ike.

And here. Don't think not, said Nia. But...our ancestors...?

Scum of the earth, said Ike. Wreckers. Pirates.

Yes, that's us...

Rioters, added Nia. Had to call the militia in. Riot Act read and all...

A thousand wrecks on this coast, said Nia. First is documented 1500, or something, I'll have you know. But must have been thousands before that...

Course...

Look, I get all that. I mean ancestors. But first of all the people down here... The first people...?

Hiding from hyenas?

Or...?

Wolves?

And each other.

Sounds like each other. But yeah, wolves. Hyenas first. Wild dogs? Well, wouldn't you?

The plague, said Skye.

Conscription, said Ike. Just about anything. He dropped another stone into the darkness... The three craned forward...

XIX

Skye seemed to be sleeping. Nia and Ike sat together where the tunnel divided.

Hey, she said. Tell me more about...

Not bloody Johnny Tarr, I...

No. Remember you told me about Niamh.

Yes.

You were hungover.

Rest of my life...

What?

How's big sister?

Exhausted.

How much older than you is she?

...Only about eight years. But so what...?

Just working things out...

Yes, well, okay. But so what?

Nothing.

Ike made himself more comfortable, stretching out his legs.

We'd get the ferry going north. Me and Niamh. *Noord*, yeah. On the *Noordster*. Only about ten minutes. Get off and walk into the derelict docks.

Why?

Why not? Exploring. Like here.

Course.

Interesting place, about to change. On the cusp. Maybe like The Caib but much bigger.

Not everyone likes what's happening here, said Nia.

And some do, added Skye, waking.

These new bars?

Better than before.

The Cat?

But it doesn't sum us up. And surely it's different now...

Anyway, said Ike. Noord was huge areas of empty warehouses, empty car parks. Everywhere the graffiti artists were busy...

I remember New York, said Skye. Didn't seem anywhere they couldn't reach...

Could be raw in winter. Once or twice Niamh said no, it was too cold. So we'd stay close to home.

Round here it's March, said Nia. February fill-dyke Siân called it. Slacks brimming... Yes, snow too.

But sometimes it worked, said Ike. We always headed for this particular café in the corner of a warehouse. Wood-burning stove, old wrecked armchairs. If it was cold, we'd choose rum. If warmer, yes, beer. *Butcher's tears.*

Sounds great, said Nia,

Felt like the start of something. Decent people mainly. Okay, some wrecked old hippies, but what's different? Ever.

Or punks like Sinbad, smiled Skye.

Yeah. Sometimes I looked round, expecting that red hair of his, bobbing about...

Kick out the jams... laughed Skye.

Might turn up yet, said Nia. Ooh, who's that bloke with the oxy lance?

But it was Niamh's type of place, continued Ike. Squats, you know?

Did you live in a squat?

No, with friends. But they were never there.

Great.

Yeah, good place. Being developed. Money, see…

Like here. Now.

Yeah. World over.

Saskatoon, Skye smiled. Boy, the Barry Hotel. Had to go, I suppose. Kind of a relic. Not that Canada has many relics. Sad in its way.

Ike looked around. And you know? You know…?

What?

I think Niamh would like what you're trying to do here.

Wow. Is that a compliment?

With your Indian stuff. The local…er… the organic…

Getting through at last?said Nia.

So maybe when you asked me about this half-arsed scheme, I thought, I thought…

You thought she'd have said go for it.

Basically, yes.

So, we owe it to Niamh. She's been civilizing you. 'Bout time, boyo.

So we'd cross over.

On the ferry?

On the ferry. Only way. For us. Could have driven, but no car…

And…

Shake the rain off.

Those *Butcher's Tears*, laughed Nia,

And yeah, share a couple of Butcher's. Or maybe more than a couple.

Or rum? said Nia. I hardly ever sold it in the Paradise…

Rum sometimes. In the cold. Strong stuff but we weren't driving. Thank you *Cap'n*. Ferry was free…

Was she…?

Ike grimaced. Ill, you mean?

Well, yes.

Didn't know. But, looking back there might have been *signs*… Pains. Discomfort. I thought it was hangovers… *Christ*…

Don't blame yourself.

Ike stood up. Of course I don't fucking blame myself.

No, you shouldn't.

Don't worry, I don't. It was cancer. It was unstoppable. It just roared through her. But I tried with the oil. Every night, her golden bath. Candlelight, all the oils. So many nights…

You loved her, murmured Skye.

Well, I never told her that.

Oh…

Who could say?

Well, you might have, said Skye.

Okay. Maybe. Yeah. I might have loved her.

Course you did.

Might have? shrugged Skye. O Christ…

Yeah. Okay. Point taken. And I'd sit on the wet floorboards breathing in that elixir. Holding the big rough towel she liked.

Like an old rough dog. Ever had a dog like that?

Ike looked around.

But didn't work, did it? It didn't work.

XX

It had happened so quickly. Ike set off and Skye followed. Hardly a glance back, and no high fives with which the expedition had begun. What was she supposed to do but begin her crawl into the darkness? Ike was adamant it was the best way back. Nia couldn't see how he knew that, but her own sense of direction was never acute.

At least she was fit. Pushing a buggy helped with that. Uphill, on the rise out of Cato Street she always put her back into it, shopping in the tray beneath, Ffrez's gear in a backpack, wipes, snacks, those dried banana flakes Ffrez loved. Have to buy more. They'd brought them down here too. Bananas underground. Tropical Shwyl.

Nia could see her daughter now, at home with Serene. Ffrez liked to explore the shop and maybe they were doing that together, Ffrez in the forest of scarves and summer dresses, or with one of Serene's friends who was coming in to help.

Tough kids, those girls, brought up on fairground work, tanned skin the colour of pennies, sand in their sandals, Chinese dragons or Samoan calligraphy on their arms and thighs.

Big families, usually, kids bringing up kids. What had Ike said about Ice Age people being tattooed? Maybe it had happened down here, there was plenty of room, children grooming one another in firelight, listening to hyenas outside, babies moaning with malaria. Maybe the whole population had been delirious.

Thank God for the neoprene, Nia said to herself, and maybe they should be roped and maybe not roped, but at least they were moving. She knew if she halted all she might hear would be Skye's scuffling ahead in the darkness, her belt and harness, that chinking sound, a music never heard before in this world, so close to the sand, to the main road with its sewers and drains.

But here she was. Her idea had become reality. This was it. Ike had insisted this was the tunnel that lead home.

Nia stopped crawling. *Tunnel?*

Tunnel.

Tunnel…

That was the word. That was the word the man had used. The man she had met in the dunes, the man who came out of the bushes, his face in her face, his breath mixing with her breath. Out of nowhere that man, on the path that was hardly a path, rain on the leaves, rain in his face, that face streaming with rain as if he had been crying.

Or maybe it was herself weeping, coming back from her exploration. Where the trees met, where the branches grew into one another, the steepest summit of the dunes. Where the bryony burst back and red, its ropes across the track, her rainforest she had loved.

Tunnel the man had said. *This is a real,* he'd said,
   this is a real
   this is a real
   this is a real
   tunnel of love.

Yes, when Ike had said that word Nia remembered. Remembered everything. Like a key, that word, or this dark place the key, or the way Ike said that word, his insistence, his arrogance but it was that key had unlocked her memory.

Nia tried to sit up as best she could. Skye was vanishing ahead but this was more important. She shifted her right hand, her hand in its neoprene glove and her palm closed round something she knew should not have been there. Something small, something...

Her torch revealed it was Ike's meteorite. The one he hung round his neck. On a leather thong. And the thong was still attached. Nia had listened to him describing where it came from, and recalled his words. A desert, he had said. And desolate.

From a different system, he had told them, that night around the fire. And someone had asked what he meant by system, and Ike said another solar system, another...

The thong had snapped. She didn't know if he was still wearing his undersuit. Two nights underground was enough for her. Would it be three? She hadn't shat and hardly pissed. But Nia would keep the talisman until Ike realized it was missing. And present it to their leader in triumph.

Bit careless, she'd say. Bit careless of you, boss. And Skye had passed straight over it, unaware. Hurrying to keep up. Doing the leader's bidding.

Passed over in the passageway that had stones and branches of holm oak and somehow salt-bleached driftwood out of the sea.

Ike said he had found a dried out dogfish in another of the passages he'd explored alone. Hard as a fossil, he'd said. But puckered for a kiss. Nia didn't know how that could be possible. But who knew what they'd travelled over in the tunnels. Yesterday Skye had shown her one of those plastic yokes that held beercans together. She knew there might have been a river flowing above their heads. Even in this drought.

It seemed they were crawling uphill. But sometimes the tunnel led them down. There was sand in the passage, moist in places. Already its grains had entered her gloves. Likely to be sea glass in it too, the supernaturally green sea glass she loved. Serene had volunteered to dust the sea glass scattered around *Extraordinaria*.

If she had chance to look Nia knew there'd be grains of plastic and Styrofoam under her knees. All that plastic washed up on uninhabited islands. Pitcairn, wasn't it? More than remote. That last night they camped out on the beach, which seemed a lifetime away now, there'd been a freezer on the sands. She'd opened its white door. The metal was scored but the shelves still in place. And all those wipes she tried to recycle? The cottonbuds? Well, she was giving it a go, wasn't she? But bad mother she was not. No way…

Nia unzipped a pocket and put the meteorite within. But unzipped it and checked her discovery was still there. She did this three times. Then smiled.

Christ, both me and Skye OCD. Aren't we? Obsessionally compulsive. Not necessarily, love, not necessarily. But when she'd put the icon away safely she reached out with both hands to discover what else Ike had mislaid, knowing there would be nothing.

Maybe he had dropped it purposely. As a test. Nah, don't be ridiculous. He loved that little piece of alien iron. Radioactive, he said it was. Maybe it was killing him. Maybe it would start killing her now… But poor Niamh. His little thrush…

Above her head was some kind of root that had burst through the limestone. A droplet hung from it, round as an earring. The root was white in the torch beam, white as the bryony vines that had tied the trees together in that other tunnel.

That's what she loved about the dunes. The danger. So many poisons, almost a conspiracy to kill, if you didn't know what you were doing. If you didn't know where you were. Yes, her world was venomous.

Nia's mouth twisted as it did when she bit into a sloe. She knew she was mad. Her mind was racing but then her mind always raced. But racing in a way different from other people's.

Maybe it was Ike's caffeine drink he had insisted she try. All those protein snacks. Perhaps she was going to be sick. The first person ever to vomit in The Shwyl. At least, since the Ice Age. Maybe they should be looking for bones? Human? Hyena?

It's this thinking about bryony, she told herself. The great purgative, those berries. Didn't they call them devil's cherries? All those in peril on the sands. Yes, she knew she was mad. And now she knew why...

Red eyes.
White faces.
Red mouths.

What rites had been devised around that lagoon? she wondered. What atrocities committed? She saw boys in masks, women who wore horses' heads.

Red eyes.
White faces.
Red mouths.

Nia was singing again. She sensed the invisible Skye pause and wait.

In the torchlight she saw lines of red limestone in the passage. The closer she looked the more different this place appeared.

Yes, children's faces smeared with kohl. But what was kohl? Charcoal then, lurid as lemurs those children, crawling through this tunnel on their way down, their way up, singing together in the darkness or the firelight. Forgotten music, those songs. But sung by her tribe. And she was the last one... As Skye and Ike could never be.

Warpaint, she supposed. But what art in that mascara?

Red eyes.
White faces.
Red mouths.

What's up? called the older woman eventually, her voice distant, almost suffocated.
    Nothing.
    Sure?
    The word echoed, a sound never heard before in this place.

No. Nothing.

Nia's words themselves were fossils crushed into lime. The air in the passage was stifling and her knees ached. Weird bloody limestone, she thought. Her hollow world.

But guess what? she whispered to herself.

XXI

Nia walked to the edge. They'd paused by a smaller lagoon. There was that same taste in her mouth. She swallowed but it remained, even after a suck from her bottle.

Iron, she considered. Or blood. Yes, that same tang of blood, or seawater, or a naked blade on her tongue. But darkness, surely. Creeping within her.

Black the lagoon, and still. About twenty yards across, she calculated. Looked as if it was frozen. Ike had skimmed a stone across and Nia watched the ripples. She stood on the rimstone that seemed made of calcite, mercurial, almost snowlike in her torchlight. There might have been lightning trapped within.

The others had gone to the far side but she hesitated when her beam revealed something near the edge. She took one step into the water and picked it up.

The touch thrilled her. Yes, metal, surely, and not driftwood. This was manmade. Thick with sediment, it had been sealed with duct tape.

Her fingernail found the tape's edge which she began to unwind but suspected might be yards long.

It proved to be a tiny stainless steel flask, branded with the word *Chalice*.

She opened it and saw a tube of paper thin as a cigarette. In blue ink on the lined page was a date, 10/12/14.

"This is our prophecy, made when our world is ending. There are so many storms now. You will understand this. Because if you are reading, you have survived. You will be one of those challenged with making the world again. A new world that has always been foretold as part of the prophecy."

Foretold? Oh dear. Somebody had been reading Tolkein. Nia thought she knew the date. A famous winter of hurricanes, of tidal surges, of experts forecasting erratic weather. Much of the driftwood now in The Shwyl would have been washed in by one of those tides.

The Arctic was melting, people said. The Antarctic breaking apart. Petals of a rose. The current heat wave might be linked to the problem, but the only reason they were underground was this year's drought.

Crusts on the slacks, sand thick with sow thistle. Signs? She didn't know. Nia licked her lips and there was that taste again. Iron, yes. Didn't her mother complain of a taste when she took her medication? Those white tablets, day after day... So small but they weighed her down. Lead in her steps. Everything too much trouble. The side effects were destroying her.

Oh, the weight of the world. And Siân's lips always dry. That atrocity of thirst.

The flask would have been filled with drops from the Chalice well at Glastonbury. She was still thinking when Skye came shuffling up behind her, holding her close, reading over her shoulder. The older woman examined the flask.

Wow.

Yeah.

Mm. Not bad. As pagan relics go. Pricey, I expect.

S'funny. I mean here.

Yeah. Here.

Unbelievable. Reads like a letter from the future.

But...

It's our past.

Few years.

Makes me feel...

What?

Old?

Strange?

No, really is a letter from the future. Put it in the shop, Skye said. With all your sea glass. And how could we forget the hurricanes?

We haven't, said Nia. Horse's head!

Yes.

All those paintings!

Titanium white.

Remember the dunes sliced apart?

Like on a lathe, Skye said.

But your picture was on the news. She smiled but released herself, the lightning still under her feet.

Got paid too, said Skye. Or better, still getting paid...

Glad someone's benefiting.

We're benefiting.

Yes.

If you recall, we bought that hanging for the bedroom…

Okay, cost price from the shop.

Yeah. Sorry.

But the BBC didn't cough up.

Those US outfits did.

Sky too. Sky being nice to Skye.

Look, don't tell Ike, said Nia,

Why?

He's bound to make a joke of this…

Better than us bickering.

He says maybe we should go back.

Suits me. If we can find our way…

Like mission accomplished.

Aye, aye, skipper.

Well, it is. Isn't it?

Think so.

Yeah.

But what a place.

XXII

You had it, though, whispered Nia.

The women were in their kitchen, the only light a salt rock glow, illuminated faint orange. It was light Nia loved. They were selling the rocks in *Extraordinaria*. It reminded her of the pane in Caib lighthouse.

Had what? Both were sleepy.

Sask, Nia murmured eventually. The Toon.

Well…yes. It was weird, though.

Course.

Course.

But…

Mm…?

Everywhere's weird.

Suppose.

Which is good. Isn't it?

Suppose.

Tell me a story about it. Life is stories, remember.

Skye took another mouthful of *Diplomatico*.

Well, this isn't a story…

No?

This is a memory.

Are they different?

Can be. Or can be the same.

Depends on…

How you tell 'em. Yes..

Okay.

I could see the weather was getting worse, Skye said. Think I was on Third Avenue. Yes, Third.

Sure?

Sure. I caught the bus at Birk's Diamonds in a snowstorm and went to the back.

Like at school, smiled Nia. On a school bus.

Loved the buses there. Orange, I recall. With a wire you pulled for the bell.

Nice.

Well, there was a girl in the next seat, trying to open the window, struggling with the heavy catch, like the handle of a jack knife. Then she turned around and asked for help, but I said no, it was too cold. And then she leaned over and spoke something that everybody pretended not to hear. Leaned over and said *Baby* and looked at me straight. Thirteen years old with these broken teeth, a jewel in her nose. Looked at me straight and I saw the snow on my Dakotas becoming blackness...

Your boots?

Shush. And for the rest of that journey she pushed at the window that wouldn't move, angry with it, starting to cry, face pressed up against the glass and the black membrane of the storm. As if she knew it was the only way out.

There was a silence.

Oh, said Nia.

Yes.

So, a memory. Not a story.

No, it is. A story.

Maybe…

And this is still our campfire…

Suppose.

I can see that girl.

I can still see that girl. I can remember that girl.

Girl with the jewel in her nose?

Yeah.

Thirteen?

My guess, yes. That jewel like Albeirio, the double star. One star yellow, one star blue…

Mm…murmured Nia. Thank God for astronomy. Trying to get out?

Yes. Wonder where she…?

★

The orange glow from the salt rock was bathing them both. Firelight, Nia thought.

Hey, guess what? Skye murmured.

Yeah?

At her time of the month, she'd bury her blood.

Who?

Jeanne.

Who?

Jeanne. In Bud's.

Oh…her.

Yeah…Jeanne.

Right…

She drove out on to the prairie and buried it where the coyotes couldn't dig it up. Sort of a ritual. Kind of a ceremony…

Maybe we should do that in the dunes, said Nia. Dig it deep because of the foxes. Got to believe, see…

In what?

Something.

Magic?

Why not?

Stories are magic. I want to be magicked.

The solstices and all that?

Well…

Some people love… whispered Serene.

What?

Oh…the incense aromas. Everybody says that about it here. The sea glass, the Indian clothes…the lights in winter. Red and gold. But always how it smells…

Change from the slipway, said Skye.

Well, they're cleaning up the outfalls…

Shame, said Ike. I love the smell of sewage in the morning.

What did one woman, say? murmured Nia. Your chocolate, your incense and your….

Cinnamon? Nutmeg?

Jasmine, I thought…

Exotic aren't we?

Nia stepped forward. *As ambergris leaves a rich scent unto the taster. Da da da da to some degree of spiciness.*

Bravo, said Skye.

John Vine would have said that. I remember him doing it once. Somewhere. Maybe on the seafront with Siân and a bottle of sauvignon in an ice bucket. If it was sunny. But Siân always loved our seaglass. In fact, I've been dreaming of seaglass.

What don't you dream about? laughed Skye.

But remember the seaglass left behind in the tide?

You're compulsive, said Skye. So what's the word for a seaglass collector?

Dad would know. Not Siân... Ike, you definitely might. Not.

Ha ha, the man mouthed. No, seriously, what's a seaglass collector? he said.

I've brought home pocketfuls, said Nia, and filled the windowsills. Jewels, I thought. They were mine, those glass alleys...

I thought marbles too, said Nia. In school my marbles were marvels.

Me too, said Skye.

Till you both lost yours, laughed Ike.

Watch it.

Yes. White as sea fret. But some an otherworldly green... Oh yes. A seaglass green. Polished a thousand years, that medieval glass. Those...

Coke bottle glass, too.

And...

And Fanta. And those old black flagons.

Some antique Coke bottles are worth a fortune, said Ike.

No, what about those brandy bottles smashed to smithereens…

And…

It's plastic now. And the seaglass picks up dust…

Which I clean up, laughed Nia. But why do I use seaglass in *Extraordinaria?* To be discovered. Sometimes kids steal it. They think it's precious stones. And it is. Oh yes. My superlative green…

Green's not easy for a photographer, said Skye.

But think of it, continued Nia. Those thousands of women in Sonagacchi, selling themselves. Biggest redlight in India… And the seaglass scattered like emeralds around the Freeset bags… Those diamonds I found in the sand… As if I was honouring them and their work… Like the women who sew mirrors into our clothes. All those mirrors. By hand…

Maybe should be birth pills. Or condoms you scatter… But that's why I had to leave Kerala…said Skye. It's the men. Those grinning, those skinny little fuckers. Joining the patriarchy. Their inalienable right… What's another bint up the duff…?

★

You all know my phone's like a part of me, said Serene. But hey, I didn't get any calls from you. From down below.

No, said Ike. Phones were banned. We were trying to be realistic.

As in Stone Age realistic, said Skye.

As in prehistoric realistic, agreed Nia. And I missed mine most. Because...

Of Ffrez, said Skye. Course.

Three days, said Ike. And two nights. Should have been longer.

No way, *brawd*, said Nia. It seemed endless. I can still taste it.

Okay. But could have been longer? And taste? What?

Darkness. It's got...into my blood. And my knees!

We could have gone further, said Ike. If we'd tried. You were...

What?

Never mind. No, he considered, I'll say it. You were right. It could be a huge system. We saw only a fraction. But that pool, the smaller lagoon, the chambers, all need to be named. That vault we saw. Fantastic. The paths that water had created. Yeah, water finds a way...

But what if... suggested Serene.

Yes?

What if something had happened. With you being miles underground. Like in a coalmine. What if...

Skye picked up the *Diplomatico*. Sniffed its mouth, read its label.

Ever been to Venezuela, Mr Pretty?

Er...no. Can't go everywhere, can I?

Hmm. Wonder whether Johnny Tarr had a phone. Down there?

Not a smartphone, said Ike. Not like it is now.

Kind of takes the gloss off it, for you? Can't get lost anymore? Even if you tried, eh?

There was another silence.

I know, said Nia, that we weren't sure about our hands. You said, didn't you, Skye, it's kind of...*graffiti?*

The three explorers had drawn the outlines of their hands in the tunnel that was their exit, three hours before they emerged at the gate.

Six hands, traced not with a flint but with sharp limestone. Six different hands only visible in torchlight. Scratches in the stone, hardly indented.

Thousand to one no-one ever sees them, said Ike. Ten thousand. Might be underwater soon...

Think of all the cave art we've never found, said Nia. That's waiting discovery. But I still think art began in the sand. On the beaches...

Course it's all right, said Ike. But not art, is it?

No, said Skye. Not like that rhinoceros. Or the swimming deer. Painted by a true artist, those deer. The artist had *seen* those deer. Real deer, real water...

They think some of the cave paintings are best seen in fire-light, said Nia. That the fire almost serves as a projector...

But they were interrupted. Serene was speaking.

No, but do you do that too? she asked.

What?

They all glanced around.

I mean, talking about our phones...

What?

The girl looked pained. Her chin was resting on her knees. Hate the sound of your own voice?

XXIII

Warm even now, isn't it? said Nia.

Skye advanced, laying her hands on the girl's hips.

No not in front. I know, I know... Stupid.

Are you all right? asked Skye.

Yes. But not in front of...

She's only...

I know. I know.

★

Sorry to bore you, said Skye.

You're not.

You were asking me about my photographs from Poland?

Poland?

Auschwitz then.

Well...

Down there. Underground. And before. It reminded me. Those tiny cells with their eyeholes. The suffocation cell. The starvation cell...

How?

Those limestone chambers we lit with our torches. So many of them, like a...beehive... Funny how my mind works.

How?

I looked into Father's Kolbe's cell through the eyehole and wondered at the last person to peer in. Before they took Father

Kolbe away...

Well...

Like children in chimneys, I thought. The chimneysweeps who got stuck...

Look, I thought that too. Down there.

But there was only one squeeze. And the gallery at the end? Nobody has ever seen that before.

Or the cave art.

Ha!

And not cavernous, like these places can be...

It was big...

Not enormous, like I imagined.

If there's one there could be others...

Dead end though.

Who can say... Now?

The pictures are amazing...

I'm not happy with them.

Well, if you think, said Nia, we only made about three miles.

Took two, no, three days.

Three, I thought. But Ike agreed to come back.

Says he'll go again.

Good luck to him...

But not with us.

No.

I wouldn't do it again.

Nor me.

Funny, though. When you think.

How?

Taking that passageway and ending where we set off.

It's a maze.

Oh yes, most likely.

But it seemed the only way. I was sure.

Too late now.

What you say...

What? asked Skye.

About the cells. Down there...

Like dungeons, weren't they?

Yeah?

Little rooms...

Suppose...

Down there it was like darkness has been imprisoned...

And we were the first people to see it...

Blackness, really.

Yes. But not...

What?

Emptiness. No.

And maybe that...

What?

Cave art.

Lines, said Skye. Scars.

Changed your mind?

Scrapes. Scars.

Skye paused. No, she said slowly. Nope.

Nor me, said Nia. Look, there's always been sand art. Why not cave art? There's been art forever. People scratching in the sand...

Yes, always.

Though Ike said the marks were just clints.

Yeah, well...

Or made by ice...

I heard him.

But think of all the sand art that's been lost...

All your masterpieces, laughed Skye.

Art started on the beach. Not in caves. Think of those hands Ike talked about, painted in caves in Indonesia. And that rhinoceros in France...

Yes, I looked into his cell.

Who?

Father Kolbe. They made him a saint, you know.

Oh...

He's the saint of drug addicts.

Someone has to be. Most of us are druggies...

Know how he died?

No.

Starved him to death. Days without food or drink.

That's what I thought. Down there.

What?

If we had taken a wrong turning.

Dark as the ghost train, laughed Skye.

Or the Kingdom of Evil...

Was a bit like that, yes.

Used to love the ghost train, said Nia. Used to scream. All the girls screamed. Compulsory.

Then they injected him with something. After all that time

in the starvation cell...

Suppose Ffrez will try it.

Try what?

Ghost train. Rite of passage. The Shwyl was like a ghost train. Down below. I can still taste the darkness.

Me too.

But she didn't miss me much. Or that's what Serene said.

Don't be stupid.

Bad mother. Aren't I?

Stupid! You're worse than Ike. So full of himself.

★

Bloody Ike, breathed Skye.

I enjoy his stories, said Nia.

Doesn't mean I believe them.

No. Just stories.

I like his voice.

So do I.

Husky.

Kind of hoarse.

But not...

No.

Sexy, though.

Yeah.

That's it, isn't it?

What?

Life. It's just telling stories...

You know? Make a fire.

Yeah. Collect drift.

Save your kindling.

Tips of raspberry canes.

Kindle a flame.

Sunflower dust.

Sacred flame.

Sacred fire.

Course.

Praise the storytellers.

Got scared didn't we?

Scared?

Of storytellers. Called them witches.

Called them poets.

Maybe. But stories...

Stories round the fire.

Shadows on the walls.

The cave walls.

Bones in the cave.

Hyena bones?

Bear bones.

Lions maybe...

Well...

What about your dad?

What about him?

Look, there must be something.

Nia paused.

You asking about John Vine?

Sort of round the campfire.

Nia paused. Okay...

Great.

Well...a train journey is one thing I recall about...

Your dad?

About John Vine. An endless journey through London. He was talking and I was supposed to listen.

Yeah?

Shush.

Sorry. How old was I? Maybe ten. Before the big school, anyway. It was exciting, being away, looking at the streets, the brown streets, the pubs with different names. *The Hand and Marigold* was one. I asked him, and he said, don't know, sorry. Not sure. I suppose he was distracted. He was always like that. Then.

Yet I remember being surprised. No, shocked. Until then I thought my father knew everything. I was so shocked that I brought it up at home.

What's *The Hand and Marigold* mean, Dad? And he made something up, some stupid story. But I knew he wasn't sure. He was flustered, I suppose.

Why not ask me a better name? he'd say. What about *The Pillars of Hercules*? I know that. I've always known that. What about *Seven Stars*? I know that one. *The Pillars of Hercules* means...

But I was stubborn. A nagging nuisance. Yes, me and Siân always nagging dad. Tell me, dad, I'd say. No. I'd demand, I'd demanded he told me what it meant.

And from then on in our house it became usual to describe anything we didn't understand as 'Hand and Marigold'. I remember Siân telling me that dad had hand and marigolded something. Meaning forgotten. Meaning dad was stupid. Meaning dad was implausible. It came to mean dad's...what? His untrustworthiness? His...*lying*.

Funny how things like that work out. It went on for years. I was surprised once that other people didn't understand it.

Suppose it was our private language, started up that morning on the train in London, me looking out the window and seeing something. And then, of course, we stopped saying it. Like words go out of fashion. Like languages... Like people...

But that wasn't the reason for the journey. That's something that happened because of the journey.

We were looking for a grave, that's why we were on the train. Going to Bromley, I remember that... Lost in London. Lost in Bromley.

Where's that? asked Skye.

South London? South-east? Not sure.

Sarf, I'd say.

Yeah. Sarf-east, innit, guvnor. But boy, it was good to be on that train with John Vine. Yes, I was bored but I was also excited. Can you be both together? I know I was.

You can. It's allowed.

Sure?

Utterly.

Yes, in all those brown London streets. Amongst those strange pub names. On and on London went. Yes, the river I saw, but there was no sea. That's what shocked me most. All that space and no ocean.

Where's the fair, dad? I remember asking. Okay, stupid of me, but that's what I knew. Look, you've been everywhere, you're proving that. But I've never travelled. Yet. I've been interrupted, that's how I feel. As if everything has been an interruption.

You...

Shush.

Sorry.

And then it was trees, tall trees in a graveyard. But what a graveyard. Went on for miles, it seemed, those miles of overgrown graves. So much bigger than the graveyard in Nuestra Senora Street.

It was winter and dad had read a poem at a funeral. Then he suddenly said that following summer, the next year, come on, let's find the poet's grave.

And that's how we ended up on that train lost in the brown streets. In the summer in Bromley. That's always been clear. It was summertime. Before he moved to the caravan. Years before.

How old were you?

Shush! I'll always remember dad talking to me about the trees. The lime trees in the cemetery. And bees too, a wonderful summer for bees amongst the lime flowers. And the angels in that cemetery, fallen angels and falling angels, broken angels with their arms in the undergrowth, their heads hidden in the nettles.

Oh.

Shh! White and lost, those angels, with marble bibles and marble wings. Angels lost in the grass. Turning silver those grasses, like waves, I thought. There was an ocean after all in those grasses under the dew. The air here is full of salt but that London morning was saturated with dew.

I was stung, dad got stung, looking for the poet's grave. There was a man, an Australian man, who helped us. And, at last, at long last, we found it, that grave, amongst the thousands of graves.

Dad was pleased, I can tell you. I forgot about *The Hand and Marigold* for a long time. Don't know why I remembered it again. Maybe that wasn't fair. On dad... Oh well. Maybe I've never been fair to dad. But Siân, you see...Siân wouldn't...Siân couldn't...

Parents, eh?

Shush.

And I had nettlerash on my hands and on my knees. The stingies had gone straight through my jeans. But dad found it and I remember the *misty dream*, which was a line of the poem he read.

Just trying to place it...

Everything that morning was a misty dream, the silence, the angels, the grasses... I can't remember who had died but it was important to dad to find that grave.

He was a good teacher, said Skye. Everyone said. Least he cared.

Yeah, well... But I remember his face when we realised we had the right one. At the end of an overgrown aisle, on the corner... Do you have aisles of graves?

Dunno. Not a supermarket, is it?

Shut up. No, dad down on his knees pulling away the ivy. The ivy leaving scars, that's how close it clung.

I can still see the nettle blisters on the backs of his hands. All these white bumps. Like the ivy scars on the stone. And dad looking relieved as if he'd finally passed an exam. As if something had gone right. For once. And he wasn't thinking about something else.

Then we both read the poem in that graveyard. Dad could remember it, and he taught me. Because I could remember things. That famous poem and that London pub name. Oh yes, I could remember things... Then. I can't now. Since Ffrez... It changes you, you know? A kid. Mentally, I mean. Really changes you...

I believe you!

That's why I feel so strongly about mum.

Course.

Anyway, the poem was on the gravestone, the misty dream poem.

It'll come to me...

Nia laughed. It'll come to us all... But...crazy, I tell you.

Okay.

Or, just not the same.

Well...

But...about John Vine...

Yes?

I know I'll see him again.

XXIV

She blinked coming out of the sun. The bar was dark. They went to a corner seat and Ike Pretty brought the drinks over...

Look at that, he said. *San Miguel* with a good head. What a difference these glasses make. Even The Cat catching up...

Glad to be out of the glare, Nia laughed. That sand was too hot to stand on. And the big moraine? Dazzling. It hurt my eyes to look at it. Those pebbles were radioactive....

Reminds me in a way of Death Valley, said Ike. Of course, it...

No, said Nia. It's here. Our here and now. Our miraculous summer. And Death Valley? Don't be absurd...

The bar in The Cat was full of strangers. Some of the men were bare chested and teak-dark, while there were women in bikini tops. Nia recognised a few of the locals, but they had been pushed by holidaymakers to the edges of their own lives.

Outside she could hear the siren in the Kingdom of Evil, mixed in with the techno throb from The Sunflower, the cheeping video games.

Nia held her own frosted glass against her brow. Ike did the same, then looked around.

Least we're not banned, said Nia. But George has seen it all. Let's have a toast?

To Skye!

To Skyhigh Skye Hillman, said Ike. And her Caib kiss.

He looked around. Who's making the money then? he asked. Got to be considerable this summer.

Must be Manners, since Hal encountered his little difficulties.

And we're adding to the profits?

Can't beat 'em, said Nia. But we always have fair trade booze for our special events. The launch was superb...

Sorry I missed it.

You must have been in Death Valley...

Croatia. Caves there... Amazing...

This is amazing. As you well know. This is why you came home. Money, okay, a woman, okay. Or some gorgeous fellah? Don't look like that. But you knew what it was like here. And you thought, it's good enough...

Good...?

To make your stand. Can't deny roots...

You got Ffrez. Now Skye. Me?

Yes, Ffrez makes all the difference. She climbed two flights of stairs today. Those stairs above the shop. Stairs still without carpet. My little acrobat. She thinks she can speak, it's just I don't understand the words yet... But she's so intelligent...

Like her mum. Hey, you're quicker than me. Did that touch the sides? Another...?

Naughty. We're only buying water, after all. But that was...

A bit gassy. So another then?

I'll owe you.

Never thought this would be my local, smiled Ike. You know, we were scared once. I suppose. By its reputation...

Scared?

Well, put off...

Why? The drugs? The Black Lite Club? Now that was dodgy. Ever heard of it? Maybe you were wise...

Yeah, I'll level with you. That mixture of squalor and intimidation. As if they went together... The smell of petty crime. Always part of the fairground.

Like Hal's aftershave, as I remember. It's your heritage, Pretty, laughed Nia. Written right through Caib rock. Right through you.

Ike moved away to the bar and Nia stared around. It was easier now to tell who was in. A group of laughing barechested men drifted close to the table.

Hey, Petr, she exclaimed.

A man looked up. After a pause he unsteadily peeled away from the others.

Now those moobs I approve. Decent pecs, Petr. Not like some of the other specimens on show... Yeah, you're a great colour and you've lost weight, haven't you? Used to be a bit chunkier? Sorry, am I embarrassing you?

The Lithuanian smiled and shrugged and stepped closer.

Good to see you, he said.

Drinking in the afternoon? Does the boss approve?

George lets us have a drink if we tell him we've earned it.

Nia looked at the glass in his hand. If beer in The Cat had improved, vodka was stalled. Nia thought Petr would be drinking Krazy Kremlin, an oily liquid, tasting like lighter fuel. She remembered it from the Paradise Club.

But how about Mr Manners…?

He knows we work. He trusts us.

Oh yeah?

But Nia smiled. How's the reading?

Stuck in *Bleak House*. No time now, we're too busy… How many people in Dickens are mad?

Plenty, I suppose.

Yes, plenty. But how many round here?

Most, I'd say. So how's the new ride?

They're lining up for it.

I thought it might be frightening, said Nia. But word gets around…

XXV

The women were upstairs. Nia had been concentrated on the computer.

Sometimes it's all force fields and forbidden territories, she murmured.

You what?

Sorry. Chess. You know exactly where you want your pieces to go, but it's not allowed. That's why it's frustrating. I'm always taking back my wrong moves. It's the only way to learn. At least the computer allows that. But it's not like, it's not like...

Life? Hardly, said Skye.

But you were talking. About men.

Prettyboy?

Well, fathers.

Bout time he did the deed there.

All mixed together, isn't it, said Nia.

Just... What?

Delirium?

What is?

Life, I suppose,

Oh yes. Forever...

We're all stoned in our own ways. Go on, then...

Oh yeah. Stoned.

Nia checked the child alarm.

When I was seventeen, she said, I wanted to climb. Simple as that. Or, I thought I wanted to climb. And in college, later on, I managed a little. Weekend trips, just like the caving. Then back here, trying The Horns. Okay, nothing daunting in that but it made me value the basics.

You're not a real climber.

Hey, my story! But at the same time I started reading about the great climbs. So, OK, proves I was never a real climber, doesn't it? I was a reader not a mountaineer. Instead, I stared down from the precipice of books.

Wow!

Shut up. But boy, those chasms I gazed into... Used to think like that especially when I climbed at night...

Night? said Skye. Sounds mad.

I am mad. Told you before.

You climbed at night?

Believe it, kiddo.

Go on then.

So, I learned the route up The Horns and followed it by instinct. Oh, I love limestone in the dark. Its smell, that seasmell that oozed from the stone, the salt of the sea lilies, the lilies' taste. I think it was really, I suppose, really about sex...

Course it was, laughed Skye. Everything's about sex. And she stroked the girl's cheek.

So limestone makes you horny, eh? Why do you think they call it...

No, listen, said Nia. Very early on I'd learned The Horns' route. Then I began testing myself. Suppose I know more about climbing than caving. Soon only moonlight would do. Sometimes in summer it was never dark. Moonlight the colour of vodka, as Ike says about the Arctic.

Well…

Or that place in Finland he visited. Where it was all silver grey? Remember? I'd been climbing that route all my life. But now it had to be in the dark. I'd even try it sometimes barefoot.

Oh no…

Because that was important, the feel of the stones. And the smell of the limestone next to my face, my cheek against the rock.

Yes, well… Skye pulled a face. Boots, girl! Boots.

People do it freestyle, you know.

But they're mad.

And sometimes I'd lick that rock. My tongue in the crevices and the dints, for the salt of it, the seasmell of twenty million years. And the heat still oozing out of the stone as if that heat was the echo of the stone being laid down.

I like it!

Lily by lily. When it was molten. Petals of limestone. And I'd pretend to be one of the fossils, one of those shadows in the rock, an outline of Christ knows what creature.

Weird little girl, weren't you? laughed Skye. I blame your father.

Is that strange? Wanting to be a fossil? I'd squeeze myself so tight against the cliff it was as if I was part of the stone itself. Just me breathing in that limestone wind coming out of our earth. Me tasting it, the salt in the groin, the salt in the armpit. Of the stone.

Yeah, definitely sounds like sex, said Skye.

Of course it's sex. It's the best sex. Nothing like a salty groin, is there? And I knew every step, every handhold, every place where I had to use my fingernails to cling on. For dear life. My bleeding hands on the bare stone. Like razors in some places. So, no, it wasn't usually barefoot. But isn't that how a fossil clings?

Dunno.

So, yeah, I know how a fossil feels...

That's the border, isn't it? smiled Skye. Near The Horns? The boundary between sandstone and... So is sandstone sexy too?

Oh you know me. I go both ways.

Yeah, I know all about you...Wild child and then some...

Yeah?

Mad queen wreaking havoc.

Maybe. But since Ffrez, it's different. Don't want to take risks yet. Want to stay alive as she becomes this wonderful person. This miracle we made... No, I made. Now I understand what Siân felt about me. About why dad thought like that. Why he does what he does... Or did. It must have been...

And he's in Malta?

That's what he tells Siân. He depends on me to visit mum, though. Some husband...

And he's teaching?

Bits and pieces.

Sex tourist? laughed Skye.

Given half the chance, yeah. He's a bloke. At a dangerous age. You know, men who buy motorbikes, wear dark glasses.

Think they're God's gift. Think they're mysterious when they're really...

Hey, he's still your dad, said Skye.

But that picture he put up on Facebook, protested Nia. John Vine in dark glasses? In the quote dazzling Maltese sunlight? Unquote. Phony, phony! And he used to despise that kind of thing...

I thought it looked like he was on the new decking outside The Cat, said Skye. So who took the pic? Or is it a selfie? You should find out...

Oh God, said Nia. The whole idea of my father posting a selfie... But...

What?

Maybe I will. Go over.

I'll come! Fancy Malta. Not to spy, of course.

I can tell you now what he's doing, said Nia. Drinking too much in ramshackle bars. The occasional whitey.

Ike recommends Lemon Haze, smiled Skye...

Great. We're all stoners, as I say. Best way to be.

You know Siân takes morphine in that place?

No.

On the ward. It's prescribed. And, yes, it seems morphine's good for her. Cleared up the pain.

We'd all be better people if we took morphine, said Skye. I know I would... Bring it on.

But I want to check on who he's got in tow, said Nia... And find out when he's coming back. Because he has to, hasn't he? He can't just...disappear.

Bloody fathers, isn't it?

Yes.

All to blame?

For most of it?

Just about all…

★

Nia now recalled Ike talking more about his father, Dai Pretty.

Once I said, Dad, I can't make you out. Just can't.

What you mean? he asked.

Well, I said, it's like you're hiding….

Hiding? he said.

Yeah, hiding in plain sight.

What's that mean? he said.

There must be more to you, I mean. Like what makes you tick? What excites you?

You what? he said.

I mean there's work, there's family, there's…

But there must be more to it?

To what? he said.

It. Life. Well, your life…

Used to surf, didn't I? Anyway, he said, I don't get you…

And it went on like that, continued Ike. And I…I pushed him. He had his back to me and I just pushed him over. Right over. He fell across a sofa.

Oh, Nia had said. Your father.

Yeah. Bad. But I got so, I got so…exasperated. You know?

With him.

Oh yeah. I know. Same with my father. I'd really like to push him over...

Yeah, said Ike. But, in plain sight, like I said. Which meant he was kind of invisible.

Invisible?

Ike considered. Yes, he said. Invisible.

Oh.

There was silence.

What about your father? Nia asked Skye. Oh, first, was it your mum or dad called you Skye? I know you've told me before.

Mum.

So you were Sky High in school always.

Well, Hillman asks for it. That was mum. Fanciful. Her hippiedom coming through.

Yes, Skye High Hillman, smiled Nia. Ha!

Hated it. Lived with it. Still do.

She paused.

My father... she said quietly.

Yes?

Skye considered. Talked to him once, properly. Just the once, I recall. But it made me understand men better.

So? Nia laughed.

So, thanks, dad. Suppose he was saying he felt of little purpose, the older he got. Think he meant it was increasingly a woman's world.

As if. Mad.

Yeah. Mad. Said men were doomed. He meant, genetically. That one day there'd be no reason for men to exist.

Oh, I believe that.

Yes?

Got to be. He wasn't so mad after all.

Why?

Natural evolution.

Is it?

Has to happen. Course. Sex robots, you know.

They'll find ways to stop that, honey.

That's for later.

Happening now, honey.

But what did he do?

Who?

Your dad! Remember?

Accountant. Didn't want be an accountant but his dad was an accountant and believe it or not, his dad was an accountant. So being an accountant was never even discussed. Just taken for granted. Like the clothes he put on in the morning. Always these Nescafe-coloured trousers he wore. But green corduroy on the weekends.

Oh no… But comfy.

Not even that. Worn at the knees. And the crotch.

Aren't they all?

But he prided himself on keeping up with work. With new software. *Sage*, ever heard of that? Something accountants use.

Sage?

Good word. Can mean wise.

Oh yeah. *Sagacious.*

Another good word. Oh, he knew his stuff. Double entry book keeping? He was ace at that. His father used to do it by hand. Maybe his father used an inkwell. Maybe his father sharpened a quill. Well, my father had to learn the computer packages. But he said it was double entry book keeping made this country what it is. Was.

Yeah?

Straight up. Believed in it.

But you didn't fancy accountancy?

Er...

More useful than photography.

I'm an artist, darlink. Your word.

Well, who do you think are buying the new apartments? *Darlink?*

Don't believe you, laughed Skye.

You will.

Where was his office?

Old rooms in Cato Street. Not far from here. Okay, apartments now, I think. I remember narrow stairs and corners, all dark and jammed under the attic. Tiny windows, some with bottle glass. Everything smelled of damp. Black mould we tried to scrub off.

Like down there in The Shwyl, said Nia.

I remember him putting a big map over it. Didn't work.

Bit like here, said Nia.

But all gone, said Skye, now that people are looking for property. Now, yeah, now we've been discovered. It's all new decking round there...

Opening the old balconies...

But the salt gets in.

And the sand...

True, always the sand, said Nia. But what the sand conceals...

Is not what the sand reveals, laughed Skye. I know, I know...

She paused. Your turn.

Oh, you knew John Vine. Still do.

You say he's in Malta?

Yes. Maybe I'll pay him a visit... But he never... hurt me. Insulted me, yeah. But never knowingly... hurt... Look, I don't want to talk about him again, do I? Parents get boring

Yeah?

Well, I remember once, said Nia, I was on the dunes when all hell had broken loose. Helicopter, police and coastguards across the tops. Seems they were looking for, get this, *a despondent male*.

That's half the population, said Skye.

He'd threatened somebody. So all that argybargy was for him. Felt so sorry. Just a bloke out walking. Kicking up sand...

Skye smiled. I can see him myself. Hunched up, pissed off. Aw!

Yes, at least half...

Skye looked at the other woman. You go there so often, she said.

Dunes? Suppose. Well, before Ffrez. It's not big like

Saskatchewan.

That's kind of monstrous. But…still it feels little somehow.

No, where I go, said Nia, it's corners of corners. A few square feet. But every corner is different. Sand and brambles and…buried history. These old maps with *walls* and *wells* and *'remains of old roads'*. A mill. Maybe a lost nunnery…

We should frame that one you showed me, said Skye.

Oh, I'm just sad… Admit it. Aren't I?

★

Ike arrived with his flask of *Diplomatico* and shared it.

Oh oh, he smiled.

What?

Men, eh? Men again.

No.

So, what about you and Carp? he asked .

You mean sex? asked Skye.

Not something I'm imagining.

But you mean sex?

Okay.

Though what you might mean as sex and what I mean as sex are going to be different.

Oh, go on.

That's a very masculine question.

You mean obtuse?

Not necessarily.

But I've asked it now.

Ok, I'll humour you. As I recall it was only the once. Sober.
Once?

Maybe twice, but that second time was when I was groggy
with iceberg vodka.

In your blues club?

Yeah. Listening to the ice over from the river. The mooneye
fishermen calling up from the shore.

Romantic.

You're a sarky fucker, Isaac Pretty. I'm trying to be straight
here.

'Cept you're not straight.

Watch it.

Sorry. So never in New York?

Maybe not.

Not even Central Park?

Christ… You're keeping tabs, aren't you?

Just interested.

No, never there.

What about India?

Trivandrum was shitting, Skye thought now. And she realized that's what life comes down to. Like worrying about toilet
paper half a mile underground.

Neither she nor Nia had shat in The Shwyl.

As to Saskatchewan, she said, they might have found a
dream home. But could they ever sleep?

★

But… breathed Nia.

Mmm…?

You and your traveller's tales.

The salt rock glowed red. Even the sea was silent.

Well…you tell me something.

Slowly, Nia sat up.

Yeah?

Please.

Okay, this is our fire. I will, I…

But Skye had fallen asleep. Nia didn't try to wake her. Instead she sipped her rum, checked the child alarm, and thought about something that John Vine had told her.

In her father's story the name of the girl in the dunes was Arianwen. There was no evidence for this, but the name had remained important. To him.

Nia was going to call her own daughter Arianwen, but desisted at the last minute. Anyway, Arianwen was a name already taken.

For the last three years she had noted the girl who brought the donkeys to and from the beach in summer. These donkeys gave rides to any children whose parents paid a pound. The girl rode a white horse and the eight donkeys were roped together in a train.

Nia would hear the donkeys before she saw them, seven brown and one white donkey, their bridles and stirrups making the music she had always associated with the fairground. Not the pop music that had played for years on The

Zig, not the new Lithuanian techo that Petr had organized for The Sunflower, and not even Jean Michel Jarre's five note mantra that would stay with her the rest of her life.

For Nia, fairground music was the bells of the donkeys' harnesses as the train was ordered by this girl for the ride off the beach, through the fair. She would lead down Vainquer Street and out past The Lily as far as the donkeys' field.

That chink of harnesses and stirrups was the sound of climbing gear, she always thought. But lighter. Coins perhaps. The rattle of a jackpot at the slots. And forever now their equipment underground...

Or the carousel horses, Mary, Madelaine and Nathaniel. Dream horses, with the music of the mules going past, those donks led across the sand.

Nia visualized this girl with blonde hair tied back with a red rag, a mysterious someone in denim shorts and ragged tee shirt that proclaimed 'Number 9'.

She'd seen her last three weeks previously, the beach white as stubble, cider cans and a child's wetsuit washing around the tideline. But not even a shirt this time, only a black bikini top. No, a bra. And the girl's back a flame, the denim stretched across the heartshape of her arse. A tattoo on her right thigh, a capital D.

Nia failed to remember the girl in her own school. So she had walked up to the donkeys, then spoken to her on her white horse. The fetlocks were speckled grey. Big hooves shifted in the sand.

This weather, eh? she had smiled.

Love it, came the reply at last.

Look, I'm trying to work out whether we were in the comp together.

The girl made a face.

Nah. We moved here three years ago. Got the job because I came down for the horses. They were looking for someone because Cath wanted to move on. She's in the bloody office now...working with Mr Manners.

Missing out?

This weather? Course. But perfect for me. Cath taught me the stabling and the routines. All about the tides. And we were due a great summer.

The best summer?

The horse shifted.

Why not? Some people are saying. Not sure, me. Give me thirty years.

I'm Nia, by the way.

Yeah, hiya.

Nia licked her lips and tasted salt. She tasted sand. She watched as the girl rode off on the white horse leading the donkeys, their harnesses jingling as the tide approached. The cars on the Sunflower were going round, The Ziggurat blasting 'Freebird', techno abandoned.

See you then.

The girl smiled but didn't answer. A wave had brought in a bottle of factor thirty. It bobbed at her feet.

Yeah, I'm Nia, she said to herself. Whoever you are...

XXVI

Sure? asked Skye.

Yes, said Nia. I was born here. Remember.

So was I. Remember?

Natives, eh?

Sure are.

For what it's worth.

Yeah, but it's next door I'm talking about.

And I'm telling you, next door is where I bought candyfloss. For me. Now for my daughter. For Ffrez.

But the fairground's all changed.

I used to work here. Remember.

Okay, but...

Wolfs it down, doesn't she? So she gets pink all over. Does that make me a bad mother?

I just won't speak anymore, said Skye.

Cocklegirl too. Remember. All those crab sticks... And same music...

Okay.

Look, this candyfloss...

Yes?

Just like you, I was brought up on the muck... Now, listen. Here it comes... *Oxygene*, by that French bloke. Jean Michel Jarre, that's him. Those five notes.

So?

Dah, duh dud duh, daah...

Or something like that! said Skye.

Okay, I never played keyboard. So some things never change. You go with Ike. I'll get in with Iggy...

It was evening and women with kids from the caravans were queuing for the slots. The fairground arcades were loud as battery farms. A warm wind blew, there was a grain of sand on Nia's tongue, another where her filling should have been.

And you, she added, looking at Rizmas, you try this.

She passed him a tee shirt decorated in red, green and yellow lines.

Thought it would be perfect for you. And your colours, aren't they...?

Rizmas pulled the shirt over his head...

See this boy! exclaimed Nia. Perfect fit. And made in India by people who have no idea of European flags.

How does it look? he asked.

Made for you. Walk over there. That's right. Now come back...

Skinny little piece, said Skye clambering into the next car. I like more meat on my men.

Try me then, laughed Ike.

As if...

Come on, get in, Ike insisted. Petr wants to start. Budge up...

This is the highest ride there's ever been here, said Nia as she and Rizmas felt the second car judder. Must be. It's an honour for you...

Rizmas's fingers were following the colours on his new

shirt. This has to cost money? he wondered.

Present. From *Extraordinaria*. And you noticed none of us have paid for this ride...?

Well, said the boy, one good turn... Petr doesn't care. I tell you, we are making money, we are...

Minted, smiled Nia. Oh yes.

He smiled. We can't stop. All those pennies in the penny falls. Then the new plastic fivers. I never saw a fifty till two months ago. We have to be careful, and Mr Manners has bought machines to check. To see if they're...

Counterfeit? Boy, fifties in the fairground? I've only ever seen maybe two in *Extraordinaria* this past year. It's all changing, kid. I can remember when this place was going to close. Certain of it, they were. But every time there's a resurrection.

Maybe God... said Rizmas. The pair were now shoulder to shoulder under the guard rail. The first cars were beginning their orbit one hundred feet above the ground. There were crowds at the two entrances, and a queue below, snaking as far as The Cat.

Petr, who had allowed them to pick their moment, shrugged like a man who had seen everything. His eyes were pouched, the eyelids violet with exhaustion.

God?

Organised the summer. Made it all happen. My mother would think so...

What she do? Your mother?

Works in the cathedral. Polishes the brass, lights the candles. Or blows the candles out. Scrapes up the candlewax when it gets too much. And makes other candles. You know...

See. Resurrection.

Maybe.

It's important to be dutiful, said Nia. I like that.

She could feel the wind on her bare arms, in her hair. This was shorter than it had been for years. At first she'd considered it a drastic change, but Skye reassured her when she caressed the feathery pelt.

No, it's not a buzz cut, she laughed at the younger woman. It's dead sexy, you fabulous feline. You're scrumptious...

There was a hint of purple in the colour, influenced by Serene. Nia though the girl looked more striking than she'd ever seen her.

There had been screams immediately the ride began to rise. It was hard to tell if the noise came from the other cars or ground level. The fairground was now the loudest she had ever known it.

Nia inhaled the breeze and looked at Rizmas's white strands, almost hiding his face.

Why's your hair so long?

I like Iggy Pop. Don't you?

Hardly. Iggy Pop plays golf. Christ, he's a creepy insurance salesman...

No, before that... Remember *The Passenger*? I love that song. And The Stooges? They look great...

Wrecked old men, laughed Nia. Hideous. Like a thousand wrecked old men down there. They're all stooges down there. The Cat's full of stooges.

Been brought up with stooges in this town.

We play it on the ride sometimes. Because, we're all passengers, I say. Even Petr likes it... But he's deathmetal normally... Or techno.

Petr needs a weekend off. Without vodka. When's Virjilijs back?

Maybe never.

Yeah, well keep your new shirt on, sunbeam. You look good, fair play... Who you sending your money back to...?

My mother. And, yes, I have a savings account here.

Good for you. But don't tell me you're not paid in hand. Hey, maybe you should invest in the shop...?

Shop..?

Only joking, son. The pennies of the poor, that's what built this place. That's what's going into your bank account. And that's what's paying for your mum to blow out those candles.

My mum...

Resurrects candles.

She...

Knows what she loves. Lucky her.

She...

Yes. Every white van man and every Mrs white van man and every son and every daughter of every white van man and every... Christ, did I manage to say that?

White van..?

Every toffee apple. Every pint of whoosh. Every American donut. That's right. And every coin sliding down the chute. You gamble?

Nah. Well, a bit. Won a cuddly toy once.

And gave it to your girlfriend…

Rizmas brushed hair out of his eyes, peered over the side of the car.

Come on, urged Nia. Job in the fair? On the biggest ride in its history? You're a babe magnet, aren't you? One hundred percent guaranteed to pull. Some of you people in the past, you wouldn't believe the stories. One I knew, Wat, he was called, he was brushing them off like flies. Went back to Ireland in the end. Had to. Shagged himself out. Think he's got his own tribe now. Randy little so-and-so. You can't fail.

Virjilijs met a girl, a blonde girl. Next time I saw her, she was a redheaded girl. That's girls for you. Wonder what she's like now…

Pregnant. Probably. Boy, it happens. So you be careful, sunbeam. Keep it in.

Nia leaned over and squeezed his crotch. The boy laughed. Pretended to wince.

But keep your mitts off my golden trumpet. Savvy?

Trumpet?

Work it out.

Rizmas laughed. Yeah, yeah. She your best friend? he asked.

Best friend?

Yes. Skye?

Ha. Ulrikke's my best friend.

Oh. Haven't met her…

Listen, said Nia, into the wind. You know, when you answer the phone? And before anyone speaks you're sure it's from a call centre? That buzzing sound. Like a hive, I suppose. Bit like down there, maybe. Well that's what's in my ears now. A humming in my head from the call centre. Think it's altitude. Do you get it? Bees crawling over each other in a hive. You must...

Not now, no...

Look, she pointed. Over there. Far over.

On the horizon to the east Nia was following the dunes.

That's the highest point, oh yes, if I've got my bearings right. There's a wood under the ridge, as far as you'll be able to make out. A willow wood. That green smudge. Grey-green. And beside it that white place, see it? That's one of the slacks. The pools. Last year that was the deepest it's ever been. Ten foot of water. Twenty. Or so people said. Now it's dry, not a drop for months. But still a white scar like a scorch. Well, that green smudge might not look much but if you were inside, boy you'd absolutely love it.

Rizmas frowned. Love?

Because it's mysterious. Know what I mean? Hundreds of orchids. Yes, hundreds. Moss hanging from the branches, like the rainforest, like that plastic moss in the Kingdom of Evil. Oh, there's the siren! Good old Kingdom. So much screaming down there, you never realise...

Orchids?

I used to go in that wood all the time. When I was free. Before you-know-who arrived.

Your baby?

That's who. Miracle child... I'm still a virgin, you know. Still...

Yeah, Ffrez the candyfloss queen. But a very mysterious place, that wood. No name to it. Or not one I can discover. Have to make one up. Look, you can see the sand blowing across the beach from up here. Some kind of typhoon... Think that's the hollow dune where we sleep sometimes. I've always done that, and I taught Skye. Trespassing, see. Are you a trespasser?

Trespasser... What's that?

Going where you're not supposed to go. Being where you're not supposed to be.

Well...sometimes...

Course you're a trespasser. Got to be. That's us, isn't it. People who don't belong? That's us.

I don't belong here. But another summer...

No, you don't belong. That's why I like you. And why certain people don't. Certain people who think you shouldn't be here...

Yes, said Rizmas. Taking jobs... But I work, I tell the Brexit people, hey chill out...

Look, Brexit wrecks it, said Nia. I get it. But not everyone. Do you think those people would understand why I go to see the orchids in that wood? A thousand orchids with double leaves. Unmistakeable. And the silence there, so powerful in that wood. You can hear you own blood. Deep bass note. Maybe E flat. My heart in that wood beat the same when Ffrez was born. Like the ultrasound. Yes, I couldn't believe how loud that was. The music of a child growing... Oh, that ultrasound.

Never...

Wff, it's really high here. Really high. And in that wood, you can't hear this screaming... That's girls for you. Ffrez is loud, but not like some of these, not like these girls...

They come to scream, said Rizmas. All part of it. Maybe biggest part...

Then listen, boyo, if you want to be the great lover, as great as Wat, as great as Virjilijs, cultivate that air of mystery. You know?

Not sure...

Women like men to be mysterious. I do. Hey, I'm not charging for the English lesson, either.

Virjilijs has good English. Better than me. He reads books, Virjilijs. Charles Dickens? Oh very big, that book.

And keep looking, Mr Marshall. Hey, we're all still thinking about your devil's museum.

Yes?

Kind of a sexy devil?

Don't know...

At least a sophisticated devil?

Ha. Maybe...

Hey. See that other wood, just a little closer? Keep losing my bearings, going round like this... No? I'll tell you anyway. Another willow wood. That's where the emergences are.

Emergencies...?

Those springs. Dry holes in the ground now, thank goodness. You'd never guess. Where the owls live. And God, it's like the Sahara over there. That black scar where the gorse fire...

I saw the smoke, said Rizmas. Wondered what…

Now, over my side, crick your neck. Amazon Street is over there. And Cato Street down by the slipway. See? And what's that, right on the beach and above the white line of the tide? Nuestra Senora Street? Where I'm pointing…

On the beach…?

You've been there, you said. The Horns. Where the fossils come from…

Think so…

Your cuttlefish.

Think it's…

I climb there. Further on are The Tramlines. Those patterns of quartz in the sandstone? And a bit closer is The Chasm. If we were nearer it would be a green gouge, really deep. Like a wound. Where we all used to swim… Easy to drown there. Be warned.

But, it's…

Yeah?

Like a drone up here sometimes.

Drone?

Russian.

Russian drones?

Yeah, Drones. Over the forest…

Oh…

Always looking…

For what…?

But I don't swim, whispered Rizmas. I'm from a different country. No sea, no beaches… And not this wind…this wind…

Look at the beaches. Best in the world. There was one wreck, just there, the locals cut a woman's fingers off. After she was washed ashore.

Why?

For her rings, of course. Remember that. Right, there's the seafront. You know the alleyway? That's Frolic Street. But I still can't see the shop. Or the gay brothel as it was once described... True. Some people eh? Bet they voted Brexit.

Yeah, well. I tell them chill out. I tell them...

...Over there's Cato Street again. Yes, the breeze. Gorgeous, isn't it? Like a warm bath. Warm as Ffresni's baths... Boy, she loves bathtime. Every night... We get the paddling pool out every day in this weather... But how marvellous she smells. You know? Have you ever smelled a baby? No?

Er, no...

The best smell ever. Greatest thing I'll ever do...I love to just breathe her in. Deep breaths. I've asked Serene to bath her tonight. They get on so well, you know... Her skin like rosepetals. And look, I'm not drunk, so don't think that...

I don't...

We only had a quick couple in The Cat. Serene likes it. Your boss, Manners, was in. Checking on his empire... But what a creepy place... I used to work there, you know. Like everybody else from round here. And to think they've improved it. Boy, it used to be scary. Still is, maybe. So don't reckon I'm that. Drunk, I mean. Skye says I drink too much, that I picked it up in the Paradise Club.

You drink?

Not really. Skye says I spent too long on my own. Working too hard... No wonder, she says... Yeah, you look good in that. We've a new display in the window, all this stuff in from Kerala. Ordered it three months ago... Planning ahead, see. Got to. Just as the heatwave was starting. Genius, aren't I?

Yeah!

Okay, there were indications on the long range. But I took the big risk and spent money we didn't have. All these cottons in gorgeous colours and if they don't sell this year we'll never sell anything... Yes, the shop's having a good year... You'll have to come over, arrange it with Virjilijs.

Yeah...

Because we all worked in The Cat or on The Ziggurat... Brought up doing it. But look, if I had a tattoo, what would it be...

Rizmas sucked in his cheeks. In the car ahead Skye and Ike were trying not to rub shoulders.

Ironwolves?

Well... I'm not a bad mother. Don't think that, don't you ever think that. But it's hard, you know. I never thought. Everyone now, oh, boy, steep isn't it. Could be Orlando here... Wow! We're better than Disney. How high is this? How high? How fast are we?

Fifty feet above the ground. Max.

Oh yes! Wonderful.

Red eyes, white faces, that's what we sang. *Red eyes, red....*
Red eyes?

Over there. And down there. Under it all. Underground.

Yes. I heard you talk...

But look at the palm trees by the dinosaur park. Brought in two years ago and now they're in flower. Who would have thought palm trees had golden flowers?

No palm trees in Druskininkai...

Yeah, big bushy wigs. Two years time I'll be on this with Ffrez. Ten years and she'll be with her friends. Mummy, you're not allowed. Will you be working here then? Say you will...

I will!

Good. Think I like you... You're prettier than Iggy. Hey, I could have *Ironwolves* too. On my arse? It's big enough...

You...

Or what about Ike? Mr Isaac Pretty to you. He's got, ooh, are we coming down...?

Nia held her breath, then began speaking again.

So that's proof you can't see the shop from The Sunflower, but I looked, I looked... Yeah, I went with my dad into those dunes. He told me he used to ask his dad, who was also called John, to... *Ooh,* that was steep! To empty the cigarette ash out of his trouser turn-ups... Yes, all this ash that my father discovered when he was riding round on his father's feet. Like Ffrez is doing to me... Why should I think of...

Hold on tight, said Rizmas.

Ooh, yeah. Nia clutched him.

We're starting to come down, said Rizmas.

Feels like it. As long as it's not a crash landing. Don't get long, do we? That's Manners' skinny time, that is.

We could do it again.

And the caravans, see. Hundreds of vans where the sand used to be. Yours isn't much, is it?

My caravan?

My dad used to live over there... For a while. But my gramps, I'll tell you, he had this illness. Yes, malaria... Came back from the war with malaria...

What war?

Yeah, my dad used to say this place is fevers and dreams. Fevers and dreams.

Dreams?

Pillow soaked in sweat, he said. That was his father. Wet through with his annual delirium. Only twenty, cutting a path through the jungle... He thought everyone here had it, my dad. In a way. Maybe I got it... Maybe my dad... Delirium in my genes... Maybe that's one thing my dad said was true. Not Manners, though. Never Manners...he didn't have it... Don't think he's ever been delirious. *Ooh, hold my hand...*Tight! No, this would be too much for Ffrez... She'd be sick... Maybe I feel sick... Maybe I've got malaria... Maybe I'm delirious...

Rizmas circled her with his brown arm.

Look, you ever talked to Zeena?

Who?

Madam Zeena? Her by the Kingdom of Evil? No?

Don't think...

Think I'll call in on the way home. If I survive this. Cross her palm with silver if there's no queue. What's she charging this year? Oh, I know what she'll say.

What?

You've been in a dark place. A very dark place. Where no-one has been before.

Underground?

I'd go just to test her. Impossible to guess, isn't it? That. Impossible.

Guess?

I've called in once before, you know. To see Zeena. All the girls used to try her out... Which boys we'd... Don't think she's the same Zeena now... Can't be... Can she...? She seemed ancient then... Everything changes, Iggy...

Nearly there...

Oh, say goodbye to the sea. Never seen it so... Didn't Homer write about a sea like this? My dad said something about that... But people aren't going in now. With the swarms of jellies... With those weever fish. Is anyone in? That's the weather, that's...

Ready?

There was a sunfish last week. Huge great... Ever seen a...

Rizmas grasped her free hand.

Blown up like a plastic bag it was. Huge sunfish.

Coming down...

Can't believe I haven't been sick. Still time, though...

Hold on...

Goodbye sea. So blue. Goodbye grass. Red as brass. Ha! But listen, why is it girls...who want to know..? Oh. Oh...*wff*...

Are we...down?

Not yet...

But almost?

Nearly.

Are we…?

Nearly…

Oh…

Now. Yeah…

The boy stopped holding Nia. Skye and Ike were already stepping out of their car. They were laughing.

Then tell me…

Yes?

Why is it…

Yes?

Why is it always girls? Those screaming girls…who need to know…

Yes?

What happens next…

XXVII

Sometimes, said Nia, when I'm doing the orders for *Extraordinaria*, I play chess against the computer.

I know.

Real quick games.

I know…

Always white, not sure why. And the level of play is…fair. Only fair.

Do you cheat?

No. But I have to be pretty rapid, see. Can't bear slow chess. Haven't time.

Course.

But also because I don't like to feel the software thinking. Gives me the creeps when the computer takes its time. Because it's calculating how it might destroy me. I suppose that's how AI will finally win.

It's coming, said Skye.

AI? Can't keep it out.

Nia nodded to herself.

Anyway, the best part is when my white queen gets behind the black pawns, breaks the black defences. Then she can run amok.

Wow.

Yeah, my psychotic queen on a killing spree. Black knights and black bishops trapped. Then slaughtered, ha ha. My victory over the computer, which is a much better chess player than

me. But better only when it takes its time. When I give it
time. But that mad queen is the real me, I think. Bloody and
hysterical.

Yes, think I know already, smiled Skye. But we're all like
that really. Do you save the games?

Um...

Pity. I'd like to see you at your maddest.

Yes. My murderous side.

Scary.

You know, I chose a Scandinavian voice for the computer?
said Nia.

You told me!

She's called *Ulrikke*.

I know! You whisper her name in your dreams.

I don't.

You do. *Ulrikke, O Ulrikke...*

Don't be stupid.

Nia paused. Do I?

Think you did. Once. But only once.

Well, she's dead sexy when she says 'checkmate', smiled Nia.
The cow.

XXVIII

My genial spirits fail,
And what can these avail?

She was digging in the sand. It was part of an excavation in one of the tumuli and was going to be on the news. After three thousand years the locals were famous. The weather was hot and John Vine was digging too, a spotted sweatrag round his brow.

And even Serene was digging, her hair purple as it used to be, long-legged Serene, breasts loose in her purple vest, and others too, strangers she'd never seen in the dunes and a woman shouting 'here, come here...'

She pushed her way to the front of the people digging. There was excitement as the woman brushed sand from the stones she'd uncovered.

'It's another grave,' she heard her say. And there she was, the girl buried in the dunes, the girl's bones laid out in the direction they'd predicted.

South-west, the woman was shouting. It might be a girl. Because always the dead were young.

Driftwood, this girl's legs.

Pelvis a pale saddle.
Skull scoured white.

She could imagine her possessions:
Cuttlebone brooch
Goatwillowstick
Jay feather in a purse.

But no gold or jewellery. She was no aristocrat. She was a cocklegirl
from the fair, wasn't she?

When she was a child these had been her toys. She was that child,
asleep in the sand. A fossil in the dune. And now when she looked
down it was herself she saw in the grave.

★

Since Ffrez, time's been chaos, said Nia. Life was never like
that before. And I know I'll never get it back. That orderliness.
My routine. That feeling I knew where I am. Who I am.
Because I don't know where I am now. Even though we're
out of The Shwyl and won't ever go back. Will we?

No, said Skye. I never guessed you'd hate your own idea so
much.

It's like the carousel, the first time I took Ffrez around. Even
though she was crying – no, sobbing – I stayed on with her.
That was on Madelaine, she was always my horse, even all
those years ago.

Ah...

My silver Maddy, going around in that Saturday afternoon light. Then suddenly, it's me with Ffrez...

A new generation in the fair.

I remember Siân once on the next horse, yeah, my mum on Nathaniel, those years ago. Used to think I could stay there all day. Loved it. Everything going round... I even recall the song they were playing, *Puppet on a String*. It was ancient even then but Sandie Shaw's still gorgeous. Isn't she?

Miraculous, said Skye.

Siân and me on the horses, the dream horses... But Ffrez, poor Ffrez, she was outraged when it was her turn. Yet those years ago I stayed on until Sandie finished and the horses slowed. Siân had to pay twice. Poor Ffrez. Am I a bad mother?

You're a great mother.

But...

Yes?

I'm just not sure anymore where I am. I'm still going round on that silver horse. Maddy and me. And you see, you see...

★

One minute Nia was behind the counter at *Extraordinaria*... Or maybe it was The Cat....? But now she found herself in the sandhills. The air was so warm she had decided to slip outside. Wasn't Ffresni with Serene in the yard, playing in the paddling pool? Or with Skye in her studio? There were two missed calls on her phone. Both in the last minute. But the phone had not rung… No emergency then.

And suddenly, here she was, listening to her sandals on the chalk, then through gravel. Then suddenly silent in sand. The light was shattering. Maybe Nia had never seen light such as this before.

She rubbed her eyes and squinted. The dunes were dazzling but seemed to lie in bands. Horizons of colour. She closed her eyes and looked again. Gradually she realized it was flowers she was seeing, the yellow, the purple, and all that blue. Somehow she could feel the colours, sense them reflecting on her skin. The orchids were coming out of her fingers.

It was as if she was a mirror, one of those glasses she recalled in the fairground years before. Her body swollen, her face stretched…

How she had stared at herself then. Ugly and impossible. As if she…

Perfect, she thought. No sunglasses, no lotion, nothing on her skin. But there was a pulse in her head. That sudden sunthrob. Squeezing her eyes shut, she tried to focus again. Black now. But dazzling darkness. She'd brought the darkness with her out of the ground.

Maybe the funfair was behind her. But there was no sound. It was confusing. Yes, she was going round on Madelaine, faster than she'd ever thought. Going round with her eyes closed yet the light like a video game, one of the new ones in the arcades that cost so much. Another of Manners' big ideas...

It was hard to keep up with the play. She'd seen boys doing it, some would stay all day. While Serene, yes, Serene was good too, taking aim and the bodies exploding into so many pieces.

Blood, she thought, so much blood. And here they come again, those creatures...

Yes, sand. Under her feet. And the thyme in its horizon a mist she disturbed with every step. She thought it must be thyme. Was thyme purple? In a purple haze. So who'd done that? Dad would know. Yes, thyme, going on forever. Like the sand.

★

Low that night was a sandhills moon. Fat above the corals of the crests. The dunes were riven by parallel valleys and some-times it was difficult even for Nia to grasp where she was in that tiny, epic world.

Usually she relied on botany and geology. Winter was the most difficult time. The slacks were predictable interruptions, but since pregnancy and Ffresni, she had not visited. Only now was she reacquainting herself.

Yet everything was different, as she knew it must be. That was life on The Caib. Nothing stayed the same. Never sand and not herself. But she regarded the moon. A pheasant's eye, she thought. Her father had told her that. Another quotation he was using as his own. As always, he was dependent on other people's words to justify himself. So how could anyone believe...

★

She tried to find the place on the beach where she and Siân had their greatest disputation. Ten years ago? Fifteen? Or was it more?

Nia had told her mother she would be with friends in the dunes east of the slipway. Home by eleven at the latest, she had promised.

When Nia didn't arrive, as the girl knew would happen, Siân had gone searching. The mother had driven up the track on the dunes' edge and found a fire. Isaac Pretty had been one of the older boys, but the other girls had seemed a year ahead of Nia.

All told there were about ten children, drinking, singing, cooking over their driftwood blaze.

Nia Vine! Siân had gone round calling. Anyone seen Nia Vine?

No-one co-operated. Siân became enraged. When Nia was revealed she demanded her daughter return with her. The girl had not agreed and there'd been an argument. When Nia continued to refuse, Siân had seized her by the hair and tried to drag her to the car.

Nia had been amazed by her mother's strength. The child was lifted off her feet, screaming and tearful.

Incredulous at Siân's determination, Nia could still remember the pain in her scalp, the taste of her mother's hand across her mouth, the sand that stung.

Then her own face was being crushed into her mother's salty breast as the two had fought.

You will! You will!...was the phrase Nia remembered her mother shouting.

You will come!

Mortified, Nia had given up. She could feel Siân's strength and was physically afraid. Of her own mother. Perhaps that was the first time she had wondered about Siân's stubbornness. She'd never seen her like that before. Maybe that was the first breakdown.

Not that Nia was different. She had refused to speak to her mother for a week. Eventually John Vine had called a family truce and both women turned bitterly on him.

It had ended in further tears, the best wine in the house, and Siân unconscious after too many glasses. Nia always remembered it. Her disastrous family.

Once Nia had blamed herself for provoking her mother. Now she suspected it signified something else. But where had Vine been that night when Siân was performing a father's role? John Vine had surely been off at another event with his latest leading lady.

Wasn't he always hoping to discover a new Sylvia Plath? One of those neurotic kids with long hair and longer legs? The English teacher who tried too hard? God, he'd been so transparent...

★

She had sometimes visited the crests at full moon. When she was thirteen? Yes. Fourteen? Yes. Sixteen? Maybe. Seventeen? Maybe she had made the effort. Usually a friend came, but once the adventure was solitary.

After they were made, the trips were never forgotten. Once, a hunter's pink moon, once orange, and on every other occasion a white moon. But, full moons. How she was drawn...

Nia imagined looking down from the moon's surface. From the shadowlands that lay there. Pitted like pumice, someone had said. And the dunes were similarly cratered.

You're no different, she'd say from the crest. With your seas of moondust. You're no different from us. Down here in the sand.

★

Yes, once every summer at full moon she'd climb. Nia liked the highest ridge, the fossils in its sand, the corals that clouded the chalk. On every moonwalk she found herself shivering above the beach, remote from the driftwood fires of the trippers, the cries of those camping out all night. As she had learned to do. As she still did.

Her gang used to organize Krazy Kremlin and a slab of whoosh. The usual rites of passage on The Caib. That loser

Cranc was bribed to buy them. What was that club? The Black Lite? Where some of the girls…Christ. Maybe John Vine suspected. But never told Siân.

★

On her last full moon walk, Nia had been yes…sixteen. The moon this time had been pink and enormous. People had begun to call these 'super moons'.

First, she felt she didn't want to go. Then she decided she must. Vine said he had to attend one of those hopeless poetry readings in the top room of The Lily. She had been to one. He was welcome to it. Maybe that bloody Rachel would be performing. Trying out her Christina Rossetti number, *I was a cottage maiden*? Give us a break. Meanwhile, Siân was at choir practice.

What was it with those teachers? Simon Middleton, for instance. Dad hated him but Nia couldn't see why. And Miss Prothero? Rhiannon Esyllt to be precise.

There were girls Nia might have invited out but somehow she couldn't organise herself. That's what her mother used to say: Get yourself together! Enough dreaming now.

Nothing wrong with dreams, mum, she always said.

There she was in an empty house. And, yes, she found herself enjoying the experience. Of being unorganized, indulging in an untimetabled hour. God, living with teachers. Both parents on their own guilt trips.

But instead of luxuriating, she had gone out. Almost in a dream Nia had caught The Caib town bus at 8pm, alighting at the top of Vainquer Street beyond the fairground. She walked through the estate and took the footpath into the dunes. No more than an hour, she told herself. The track led east with the sea on her right.

And there it was, the moon, red in the south. A rising moon with its tattoos. And daylight still strong. She found purpose, her steps silent in the sand, dew already at her ankles.

But Nia had begun to regret her impulsiveness. Her arms were bare and there were brambles across the path. She was still thinking of what the gardeners had said in the allotment. There they'd been, the usual two but in straw hats. That other hot summer, years ago.

The hats were surprising. All afternoon, those two drying their elephant garlic, picking the blackcurrants under the netting, digging majestics, their redskin of choice. Though they said they might recommend black orkneys.

Because Siân had not netted her currants the woodpigeons had feasted. The gooseberries had also failed. At least there were three sunflowers at the far end of her plot. But it was a poor year on the whole, compared with some.

The two in straw hats hated sunflowers. Take too much water, they reasoned. Greedy. But their sweet peas were splendid, and the orange splash of nasturtiums a shock on their sward.

So, not without poetry, those two, she'd thought. But randy

old buggers. Couldn't help themselves, could they.

Stylish, she'd called, after their greeting.

They doffed their hats.

Where's your mam? called the one who usually talked.

Choir, she'd called.

What choir's that then?

Oh, you know...

And your dad?

Oh, he's never home.

Nia showed off by jumping over the stile and making her way to Siân's plot.

Got bellringing myself in five minutes, shouted the other one, as she came over.

What are these then? Nia asked.

Aubergines. Doing well. This weather, see.

Dark flowers, she saw, from black stems. And the fruit coming molten out of the earth. Black lava.

Had the idea, last year, said one. It's working so far. *Eurydice* this one's called in the old catalogue. Tracked it down.

Both were about sixty, she thought. Or maybe pushing seventy. Seventy-five? How could you tell? Still men, though. Men were men while they had a pulse. Couldn't help their leers out of turnip faces. Grinning with goat's teeth. But keeping busy.

What had Shakespeare written? she wondered. Goats? Goats and monkeys? Othello, year twelve. Something about a black ram. Who was tupping? How many words meant? That? Never heard it now. But obvious. And didn't fuck mean to plough?

Fair play, po-faced Prothero had told the class that. Dropped the word in naturally. Pebble in a rock pool. All around Nia there had been an intake of breath. Maybe unfair. Rhiannon Esyllt wasn't so bad. Yes, hope she stays the course. Heard Year 9 was giving her a hard time. Little bastards. But ploughing, I ask you. Where's the pleasure in that.

Not so bad, though, the codgers. Wonder if... Yeah, probably. No, definitely. Cocks like cabbage stalks. Or radishes, as mam said one evening after wine on the seafront.

Sour fruit, she'd sneered, upping the ante. Siân had been free from school, the wine bucket before her, ice spilled over the table. Its rubble in the sun.

*

The grass had grown thicker, nickel in the silver, those grasses uncut a hundred summers. And the bracken green. Irises like lances on the edge of the slacks. Indigo rising.

The path was steeper, the moon now at her shoulder. That night, there'd be a red beach. The pools would seem full of coral weed.

Soon Nia was climbing through hazel trees and ferns taller than herself. One of her places, she thought. Yes, her father had spoken about it but now it was one of hers. She was sixteen after all.

Yes, one of mine, she said to herself. One of mine, one of

my…and she forced herself not to pause although it was steep and the summit not in sight, one of mine, one of mine, and the path turned to the left under the hazel leaves above the wartime valences with their graffiti about that girl but who could ever write such a thing and the dune slope opened out and there were orchids at her feet, drops of blood, and what was the story John Vine had told her?

A hawk, yes, a sparrowhawk. That hawk overhead had taken a songbird, maybe a yellowhammer Vine had thought. A drop of blood had fallen to the sand. He had seen it coming, a speck out of the air and Vine had found that drop. Yes he'd discovered that droplet. Or he said he had.

The sparrowhawk had flown its prey to a branch where it might devour the bird at leisure. But a drop of blood from the sky, yes, he'd told her, that lethal bird, the…

Liar, she thought. *Liar, liar.* But one of mine, one of mine, and taller than she'd ever seen the ferns about the path, almost no path at all, not if you didn't know.

The briars had to be twisted back or stepped upon and stupid, yes, she should have known, should have known, their thorns were curved like dogteeth, or talons of the sparrowhawk.

Nettles too, taller, enormous, the nettleflowers in beards she saw and she must be bleeding but no, don't stop even though her heart...

Was bursting. But she was at the top. At least, where she always permitted herself to pause. Before the ridge. Now, over the sand. Over the last twenty yards of chalk to the crest of the dune. The last limestone. The fossils and the coral less than an echo of what had been. The coral of the crest.

Because hadn't John Vine told her the sea once covered this place? Typical Dad story, how could you disprove it? The sea, the sea even before the sand was here? Let alone the fairground...

Nia had felt she might open her mouth and drink the wine of the moon. It seemed that close. A pink drink. A girly drink. Cherry brandy? Lambrusco girls? Ah, those pop tart from school. With their fags in their bags down smokers' alley, and yeah, who was that bloke who bought the cider? Yes, Cranc. Still around the fairground, wasn't he? What kind of life...?

And those girls. Her friends. Kayleigh and Kylie and Shawney and Shannon and Keely. Take a bottle up here and talk about boys. It was fun. And once, no, twice she had shown the way. Maybe it was her idea.

But no-one else would have dared. No-one could have known. Must have been her plan. The path would have been easier then because the girls would never have thought otherwise...

Even horny Shawney would never have. Been brave enough. To come this way.

★

Maybe it was clouding over. Bare armed, she had felt a breeze. One drop, two. Nia remembered it had been raining one evening when the family was swimming near The Horns, Dad, Siân, her brother, Brychan. The raindrops had been the same colour as this moon. Burnt rain, drops full of sand, rain that burst the Sahara over their car, every fat and dirty detonation. Red rain from the south-east falling like pennies, she and her brother floating on the shoulders of the swell and opening their mouths to drink the hot sky.

John Vine had shown his children a drop of rainwater, bursting it like a blister. Calling them to look. Cross when he thought they didn't care. Then lightning had exploded and Siân was gathering her brood to shelter, cursing Vine for stupidity.

Yes, it was suddenly raining. Nia paused on the return path but already the moon was hidden. Only a few drops touched her, the hazel leaves were shelter enough.

Walking downhill she realized how narrow the path was, crowded round with hazel and wayfaring trees. Seeds bright as zircons, Vine had said. When it had been his place. What the hell were..?

There was bryony too. Its gorgeous grapes. Her father had told her about the plant. Looks good, doesn't it? he said. But never be tempted. I mean it. Never.

Oh yeah, John Vine. Warning her. Wasn't that what fathers do, she'd wondered. But when had John Vine said no to temptation? All that talk in school meant... If you believed it. But even if you blocked it from your mind you found yourself believing. Picturing... As if...

No, Shawney hadn't liked the path those years ago. And Keeley had freaked, thinking they were lost. But Keeley was lost any time she moved out of that arcade in Amazon Street. They hated the route uphill, hated it down. Shawney had slipped. Her trainers were dirty.

Nia had known it was still raining. She waited in the sands of the slope. There was a bush of marjoram on the path, busy with butterflies. These were undisturbed by the rain. She'd stood where she normally did, sniffing the stones of the crest, stroking the fossil coral in the same stones.

Yes, John Vine had said the ocean once reached this height, covering all the land now visible, that coral in dead tumors and extinct suns, its stone rays reaching out of the past from the top of the dune.

She waited. Now the raindrops were enormous. She felt

explosions on the hazel leaves around her. Where was Keeley today? Nia wondered, on that full moon walk. Sixteen, she'd been. On that last walk.

Shawney had found a job in a restaurant in the fairground. Maybe like Nia she had become a cocklegirl, carrying a tray amongst the last of the gamblers on the slots, waiting outside the Kingdom of Evil until the couples flung the carriage doors open and emerged grinning, the girls clutching the boys now, some shamefaced, others truly disturbed. What better time to sell crabsticks or cockle cones?

And there had been Siân, waiting to escort her home, occasionally dad. But John Vine had found that job as a bingo-caller and it was awkward. So Donal had done it a few times, ushering her once into The Cat for her first grown up, no-parents drink in a pub.

Coke, please. How she had savoured it, the ice cubes in her chilly glass, Donal's pint, tall and smoking, on the table before her, the Budweiser beermats John Vine hated. All the atmosphere of the late summer fairground.

What had she been then? Nia had wondered. Half a mile away from town perhaps. But not a sound of the fair had announced itself. All the frenzy was being blown in the opposite direction. From the crest she had followed the tideline, a flat sea moving against the black reef. No further, she had thought. That was as far as the tide retreated. That was as far as…

But she had heard a sound in the south. She had thought it thunder, or maybe the quarry, way beyond the dunes.

If it had been Tuesday she would have known it was fireworks. Every Tuesday at 9pm a bar in the fairground set off a barrage. Must have cost a fortune, but it was spectacular.

Yes, every Tuesday. At least, most Tuesdays. Lights in the sky, rainbows, new constellations rising over the roofs. But the rumbling must have been thunder, she decided. Prologue to a storm.

Green to red, those berries, their garlands above the path. Hanging out of the buckthorn branches, out of the hazel. Out of the sky. Parasites, were they, those plants? Climbing on whatever was highest…? But oh, the gloss on them… Yet blowsy, if you considered. Old fashioned jewellery.

We'd wanted to call you that, John Vine had said.

Call me what?

Bryony. But mum put her foot down.

Bry… had thought the sixteen-year old Nia. As if. What had dad said? It'll purge you girl. Of all that ails you.

Sounded like another quotation. From someone who'd bothered to write it down. But *Bryony?* All these years and never heard Bryony before. Christ, whatever came into his head... Of course Siân had forbidden it. Bryony? A cocklegirl called *Bryony*...

At her feet on that full moon walk had been clusters of hazelnuts, blown from the branches. She selected one and crushed the nutshell between her teeth. That was easy, the shell was soft, the kernel a white embryo. Hardly bigger than a droplet of milk, she thought. Every year Nia ate green hazelnuts, each unripened cob the tip of an icicle, its milkdust cool in her mouth.

You're like me.

The man's face had been inches from her own. Nia was standing under the hazels on the climb from the crest. She had been staring into the leaves. And the man had come out of the trees. Out of the leaves in one moment, a green man, a barechested man, rank, she had thought immediately, a man who smelt of the beach and the slap of the tide against the slipway, a man made of salt, a man of sand. A man whose hair was full of the wind.

Real tunnel of love, this place, he said.

The man was so close. A man made of leaves.

Tunnel of love? she wondered.

You're like me, the man had said. You are. Aren't you? You're like me.

This man's teeth had made a ruined smile. And his mouth was bleeding. A man whose teeth were bloody stumps. As if he'd been eating. Something dead.

Maybe it was blackberry juice.

Dad had once led her up this slope. They were blackberrying. And, yes, John Vine had read that poem about picking. About blackberries. Typical John Vine. Someone else's words. Making her listen. Vine had simply launched into it, she didn't know what he was talking about. Dad, driveling on...

Not so great, was it? An ordinary poem about boring blackberries and yes, she remembered how many there'd been. Her fingers purple, her lips, her father's mouth. Like when he drank red wine. What was it? Merlot? Malbec? When Siân drank her cheeks were soon sunburned. Yes, the giveaway with mum, and Nia could always tell in the afternoons, straight after school... Siân taught only in the mornings...

And what about maggots, she remembered asking her father.

What about them? he replied. Won't hurt you. Might do you good... Worse things than maggots.

The man must have been there all the time. When she was climbing up. When she was descending. When she had decided to pause. He had been waiting for her. He had been listening to her. He had been listening for her. But what had he said? What...?

Like leaves, that man. The undersides of leaves. There were veins in his face. Thick veins. And rain, she saw. Running from the tip of his nose. Rain on the tattoo on his neck. A design that seemed to disappear down his back. A snake, it looked like, a snake with two heads or maybe it was two snakes. The snake might have been wrapped around his body... But could a snake swallow its own tail?

When he placed his hand on her breast all she could think of was one of the metal grabs in the arcades. That picked out toys for children. The toys all the children wanted. A mechanical hand. Forceps for a baby's head. The tool that had marked her daughter's brow.

You're like me. You are. I've been watching you.

There was nobody. And suddenly a man. There. Three inches away. Flecks of blood in the corners of his mouth. Pinpoints of blood in his yellow eyewhites. Maybe this was...

She had held her ground. There was nowhere to go. Her stomach had lurched but she had stayed still. Only afterwards did she understand she'd wet herself. Hot on her thighs, her own piss, then cold with everything else.

She must have passed out. When she opened her eyes she knew the world was different. As if the berries had burst. Now sour in her mouth. But she remembered the icicle that had swung above the sun.

What had Vine said? Eat those berries and they'll purge you, girl. You'll lose every drop in your belly. Every...

230

Glistening, those grapes. Some gold in the sunslant.

No, she had never told. Anyone. Never told what the man...
Won't hurt you, her father had said. *Won't hurt.* But there was
milk in her mouth. The tip of that icicle.

And John Vine had said it again. That ghost-name he thought
she deserved. Teased her with it. *Bryony*, he had said sometimes. When he was exasperated with her. When the father
argued with the daughter. And yes, she'd never been perfect,
had she? Never claimed that.

Bryony, there's an irony. Christ, he said that a few times. How
dared he? Her father, taunting...

But if he had only guessed. If he had only...
But she had never told. Never told...

Or maybe it was blackberry juice.

Notes

* All quotations from ST Coleridge 'Dejection: An Ode'. (1802).

* *Birthwort / Sowbread / Afal Daear / Esgorlys/Bara y Hwch / Aristolochia clematitis:*

A scrambling or trailing perennial herb found as an escape or a relic of cultivation in waste and rough places, often by old abbeys or nunneries, and in churchyards, woods and on grassy banks. It spreads by rhizomes. Neophyte. Grown for its medicinal properties. The date of introduction is unknown, but it was recorded in the wild from Cambridgeshire in 1685. It is now rarely cultivated, and is gradually declining.

(On line Atlas of British and Irish Flora).

Geoffrey Grigson writes in 'An Englishman's Flora' (Paladin): A strange species of a strange genus, which was introduced from central or southern Europe into the physic garden and then escaped… It survives here and there as a reminder of old practice and belief. The ancient Greek name, *aristolochia*, comes from words meaning 'best birth': Birthwort resisted poison, encouraged conception, helped delivery, purged the womb after the child was born, and repelled demons – since birth is a dangerous time when both the mother and the child are open to supernatural malice.

...The greenish-yellow flower, or perianth, constricts into a tube, then opens into a globular swelling at the base. The swelling was interpreted as the womb, the tube as the birth passages... *Aristolochia clematitis* does have an abortive effect.

Author Note

Robert Minhinnick is one of Wales' (some would say Britain's) most eminent writers. He is a multi-prizewinning poet, essayist and novelist; his essays have twice been awarded Wales Book of the Year and he has been shortlisted for the award on two other occasions. Minhinnick is also an environmentalist and founded Friends of the Earth Cymru and Sustainable Wales. The area around his home in Porthcawl is of great inspiration to his writing and *Nia* is the third in a series of novels set in a fictional community heavily based on the town itself. Seren has published three collections of his poetry, four collections of essays and his previous two novels, the first of which, *Sea Holly*, was shortlisted for the Ondaatje Prize.